Romance
&
Revolution

The First
Impression
A Pride & Prejudice Reimagining

NEY MITCH

Contents

Dedication & Author's Note   v

Prologue   1
1. The Boston Massacre   15
2. Four Years Later…   31
3. Greetings   38
4. Darcy Takes Command   45
5. Soar & Salutations   53
6. An Officer & a Gentleman   63
7. A Search for Herbs & Healing   72
8. The Worst Way to Meet   97
9. The Follower   106
10. The Next Act of Defense   118
11. Correspondence   130
12. The Intolerable Act   140
13. The Bridge & Wall Between Us   148
14. Dark Water   160
15. The Color Green   170
16. The Question That Is You   177
17. Stitched Up   195
18. Leaving the Lodge   211
19. How the Heart Betrays Itself   229
20. Another Betrayed Sensibility   235

Afterword   239
Thank You For Reading   247
About the Author   249
Also by Ney Mitch   251

Dedication & Author's Note

Good day readers, welcome to Book One of the Romance and Revolution Saga. In this tale, we find our lovers on two sides of a historic conflict, where they both have opposing viewpoints. As a result, I must inform the reader that both characters will speak bitterly to each other when they become acquainted.

Secondly, both Elizabeth and Darcy will be products of their environment. As a result, they will be very virtuous, but also severely flawed. This is not done to sour the readers views of them, but to give an accurate depiction of the times, and also to give Elizabeth and Mr. Darcy a journey that they must go on to improve. Also, this topic will be discussed further in the afterword, which I highly recommend the reader to give a look-see.

Last note, this tale will be split into two different narrative tones and voice. Whenever a chapter focuses on Elizabeth, it will be in first person narration, so the reader can enjoy the intimacy of a personal account. Whenever the narrative focuses on Mr. Darcy or another character, it switches to third person. This gives me the chance to show other events, while still having the tale focus on Elizabeth Bennet.

Also, there will be Time Travel elements to this in the very beginning.

And finally, I give credit where credit is due: my family, publisher and all who worked on this series are the best! Thank you so much and I love you. But the main thanks go to the reader who picks up this tale and gives it a chance. You're the most wonderful audience a writer will ever find, cheers!

Prologue

MEETING AGAIN... FOR THE LAST TIME

I t is a tale, commonly shared by all, that we all secretly want to love...and be loved in return.

It is also a concept that is the most rewarding thing to experience, but the hardest thing in the world to achieve. We all discover it for moments, fleeting moments, and the days roll *in and out*, as the tide of our individual fortunes bend *in and out* of formation and once more being hurled into chaos—and we lose it again. Yet, this loss is linear; it comes and goes organically.

But with me—how inorganic it is, how non-linear, and not a cause that has an obvious and logical effect or ending.

No. With me, it is a jumble, a ball of strings that is tied into complex tangles, where there is no beginning. And no ending either.

For a love to be found. To stop and to start. To begin, end, then begin again...at first, it was intriguing. It was an adventure that was unique and made me unafraid of anything that life could hurl at me. It made me brave enough for anything.

Although, that is the pain of being unique. You eventually become jealous of the 'normal'.

As I walk through the city streets, and I see the person

sitting on a bus, their face depressed as they lack significance to their lives, or they are on their phones, trying to flush out the monotony of the day, or doing everything to hide their disappointment of being single, or of never being extraordinary, or trying to suppress their violent nature—until they meet someone, and the two of them discover each other, even if the discovery is brief...yes, I am envious of those. For they will never be aware of how fortunate they are. To have a natural beginning, middle and end. That is the life!

When you become extraordinary, when fate decides that it is you that will have a journey unlike any other, the common person wishes they had your fate, and you wish that you had theirs.

That is another element of being human as well.

For some, falling in love for an eternity is all that they could desire.

For my part, I had been falling in love, losing that love, and finding it again for what I have determined—to be for five hundred years. At least. Some would find that to be the ultimate answer to their happiness.

However, for me—it made me an enemy of love. I was tired of it.

Sound...that is part of what drives us from out of our dreams, forcing us to wake, be met by strangers around us, and to be aware of how we are in public.

"Lizzy?" the bartender uttered. Hearing him call out my name forced me out of my musings, and I fell back into my environment.

"Oh, sorry," the waitress named Jenny said as she bumped

into me, carrying two trays at once and managing not to drop a sip out of any of the cups.

"It's fine, Jenny," I said, my voice lazy, as I needed time to adjust from having to tear my eyes away from the television. It was placed on a shelf that was just below the ceiling so that everyone could see it. "Nothing fell on me. Nothing ever does."

Jenny stopped in her progression, trays still in hand and she looked at me, quizzically. Next, she looked at the bartender, Clancy. I didn't have to see her expression; they both thought something was wrong with me.

"Don't worry," I said, eerily reading their thoughts, "I'm still alive and sane enough."

"Lizzy?" Clancy repeated. "Are you alright?"

I gave him a 'what do you think' look.

And guess what? The poor man had misread my expression.

"That's it," he said, lifting the remote control and about to flip the channel, "no more *Quantum Leap* for you."

"Don't you dare!" I declared, getting the animation in my voice back, and the spirit rising in my cheeks. When seeing me laugh again, they both relaxed and accepted that I was not suffering from what they called, Sci-fi syndrome. They called it a condition where a person gets so obsessed when they watch science fiction, that the rest of the world falls away and they fall down the winding road that is their fantasy. I didn't need to imagine it; I had already lived it. They just didn't know my whole story.

I had just finished watching another episode of the show *Quantum Leap* and now was eagerly waiting for when another Sci-fi show, *Forever*, was about to come on. These shows were regular watching for me and helped me endure my own immortality.

"You know how therapeutic these shows are for me," I said to Clancy as Jenny walked to the table to drop off the drinks and appetizers to some customers. Now that she saw that I had fallen back into reality, there was no more of a need to worry about me. "Some people like psychiatrists, and I've got Samuel Beckett and Henry Morgan." I was referring to the lead characters on the shows.

"You know," Clancy said, "for a pretty woman, you certainly don't believe in having much of a life."

I chuckled, looking at my white turtleneck and checkered gray pants. I was dressed plain as a dandelion; what about this was alluring?

"Or am I being offensive?" he asked, worried that he was being too direct.

"Don't worry," I assured him, "I'm not offended by a guy calling me that. In my opinion, people get too offended too easily nowadays."

"I second that one!" he declared.

"That's precisely what I feel," Jenny agreed, as she came back behind the bar, with empty trays as she began to pour some more beer into some mugs, "or they spend too much time getting offended at the wrong things."

"Oh, I have had many lifetimes of that," I said amusingly, and they both laughed, assuming that I was joking. "And that's the problem. Have you ever noticed that people are so quick to get offended by things, that they get so preoccupied with being offended by the inoffensive things, that when something offensive does actually happen, they never notice it and just let the offensive thing happen?"

"Exactly!" Clancy and Jenny said together. This made us all laugh.

"I swear," Jenny said as she put the beers on her tray, "if I see one more person get upset for complimenting someone on their looks, while ignoring another politician or a show being discriminatory, it will be the day that pigs fly. Everyone's an idiot."

"Yes, they are," I said as I began to watch as *Forever* began to come on. "And Clancy, I know you won't believe me, but I have lived enough to last over twenty lifetimes, so not having a life is the only reward that I can think of."

Clancy was about to say something, but a man sat down at the barstool next to mine and interrupted.

"There are other ways to reward yourself," he uttered with a thick accent. An accent that I was very familiar with. I didn't turn to look at him because I didn't need to.

The second he sat next to me, I felt it.

Over the centuries, it became a term that I always called it when I felt his presence:

The Rapture.

I could not describe the sensation, because it was felt, but was hard to put into words.

My body ran hot, and then it ran cold.

I became sensitive to everything that I saw, heard, touched, tasted, and smelled.

All the senses prepared me for seeing him again.

The counter that I placed my hand on was clean, sturdy and I could feel all the thousands of people who had placed their fingers where I did. I felt their urgency and hunger for any food that would come.

I heard Clancy breathing, Jenny laughing at a joke that a customer said, obviously trying to flirt with her.

I felt a fly resting on my shoe, even though it didn't touch my skin. Its buzzing was very annoying to hear at such a deafening pitch.

And the smells. From the grease and odors that came from the kitchen, to the guests who had entered. It was a warm day, so we all were sweating when we had entered, and now I knew how much the heat had augmented our aromas.

Lastly, it felt as if a gust of strong wind passed through me, the lights dimmed (but only I could see) and only his figure stuck out in my vision.

At last, knowing it was rude to ignore him, I turned to see how he looked now.

His face and figure were completely different, but I still knew it was him.

I was looking into the face of Mr. Fitzwilliam Darcy.

~

My voice should have frozen. My heart should have been seized.

But time had worn me down. I knew he would find me. He always did. So, this was just another moment for me. Despite being another first moment for him.

How different he looked to how he ever looked before.

He had flaming red hair, was only a couple inches taller than me, and while his figure was fit, it was not striking. Rather, it was comfortable, and he dressed casually. Yet, it was him. It was the man that I had loved for many a lifetime.

"Other ways?" I said with a sigh, "are you about to offer me a social proscription?"

He raised a red eyebrow.

"A social proscription?" he repeated.

"Oh, did I read you wrong?"

"No, you didn't. I'm just surprised how easy I am to read."

"And you don't like being easy to read?" I surmised, based on experience.

"No, I don't prefer that. But it's a good look for you."

"That will make this easier; I have a habit of reading people like you."

"Do you?" he asked.

"Yes, I do. Can't say I'm always right. But I do it anyway."

He looked serious.

"That was a joke," I clarified.

"Oh." He smiled and did a little chuckle that was very delayed and a little uncomfortable. I knew that laugh. "Well, what I was going to say that, it is proper to be alone, but you seem like the sort who is lonely."

"Lonely?"

"Yes. It's something that I noticed." He rolled his shoulders, worried that he was offending me. "I'm going to assume that you won't be upset with what I said, but—"

"But I'm not," I assured him, "even if you may be wrong, I am not. Because I don't get offended easily anymore, but you knew that too."

"How would I know that?"

"It's because of the way that you were when you sat down. You looked comfortable, like you had been practicing coming up to me. Therefore, I assumed that you have been studying how to do this for a little while. That could only happen if you had been listening in on my conversation."

I turned back to him and now chose to analyze his features better. His skin was a healthy peach and pink, his eyes were gray, and his nose was defined. And in his gaze was the burning passion that could melt the strongest of wills. Under that strong face was a passionate man. Also, from what I could gather, he was in his forties.

"Or am I wrong?" I asked.

He sighed.

"Sorry," he said, "I could not help it."

"Again, I'm not offended."

"Well," he responded, relaxing his shoulders, "you are very different from what I have met before. Now I feel as if I was right to be a romantic sleuth."

Suddenly, Jenny came between us, inquisitive. She looked at him. Then she looked at me.

"Ew-Ew," she said, in the way that women coo when they say things like 'James and Mary sitting in a tree, k-i-s-s-i-n-g!'. Darcy and I blushed as she walked away.

"Did she really just do that?" he asked, sipping his Guinness.

"If she didn't do that, then she wouldn't be Jenny," I replied. "She's surprised that I'm still talking to you. Usually, I'm not in the mood."

"But you're in the mood for me?" he asked, his voice husky, unable to mask his feelings.

I was not *in the mood* to make it easy on him either.

"I'm tired," I replied. "I just don't have the energy this time."

"Yes," he said, his eyes twinkling. "That's the tone. By the way, I just realized that I never told you my name. I'm Fitzwilliam Darcy."

I know, I thought to myself.

"Fitzwilliam, yeah." He continued, "not my idea, of course. It's a—"

"Family name," I finished his sentence.

"Yes." He looked quizzically at me.

"I made an assumption and ran with it," I lied.

"Well, top marks for you."

"And this is where I should give you my name, right?"

"Well, it would help," he encouraged.

"Elizabeth. I'm Elizabeth Bennet."

"Nice name."

"Thanks. By the way, you're Scottish, aren't you?"

"Yes, I am. You're good with accents. Mine is thick."

I laughed.

"That's funny?" he asked. "Good. Being funny is good."

"No," I replied, quieting down, "it's just ironic, that is all. Or quite the coincidence."

"Coincidence?" he repeated. "How?"

I looked deeply into his gray eyes, and I began to lose myself in them—again. Now *that* I was not in the mood for.

"Sorry," I said, "but I can't tell you. That's one of those things that you don't talk about when meeting someone."

He looked down at the counter.

"Well, what man does not like a little mystery with his woman?"

"*His* woman?" I repeated, amazed.

"Oh, bollix!" he hissed. "My bad!"

I chuckled.

"How transparent could you be?" I asked him.

"That was embarrassing," he responded, covering his mouth.

"Yes, it was." And when looking at him, I was utterly perplexed. My goodness, this Mr. Darcy was most astonishing. "You are so different from the others."

"The others?" he asked. "Oh, other men?"

"Yes," I rushed out, to cover myself. "Yes. *Other* men."

"I hope that speaks in my favor."

"Welcome back to Boston," I said.

"Back? This is my first time coming."

I looked back at the television to hide my face.

"Yes, bad wording. That's the first sign that you picked the wrong girl to talk to."

"Let me be the judge of that."

He followed my eyes and looked at the show I was watching.

"What's this show about?"

"It's called *Forever*. It's about this doctor named Henry Morgan. Every time that he dies, he wakes up again in the nearest body of water. Like if he dies in New York, he wakes up in the Hudson River. He's immortal. Here at Clancy's Bar, Clancy always plays the Forever/Quantum Leap marathon. At five o'clock, two episodes of *Quantum Leap* comes on, and then two episodes of *Forever* comes on. I like watching it here, rather than at home. It gives me the chance to be social without being social. Have you never seen *Quantum Leap*?"

Darcy shook his head.

"It's about a genius named Samuel Beckett. He created a time travel machine that was incomplete. Rather than traveling through time, he keeps falling into the bodies of people who exist and changing their lives for the better. Once he succeeds, he leaps into another body in a different year."

"Sounds interesting. You mentioned that they were therapeutic?"

I gave him a side glance.

"You really were eavesdropping, weren't you?"

"Well, according to you, you knew that about me."

"I did. That's why I'm not surprised."

"Why are these shows therapeutic for you?" he asked.

"Because I can connect to the characters. Especially the leads."

"One man travels through time and wakes up in other people's bodies, and the other one dies and then is reborn? You connect to them."

"If you only knew…"

"Then tell me."

Turning to him, I was about to explain further, about to fall into the very connection that we had.

Then I looked into his eyes.

The very eyes that I had fallen into so many times before.
In them, I saw another chance.
Another possibility.
But then, I also saw the end.
I saw all the disappointment.
All the pain and the loss.
And I remembered why I was alone.
"I'm sorry," I said at last, "but I can't do this."

When hearing my tone change, Darcy's eyes shifted to quiet alarm, and he was a little astounded.

"What do you mean?" he asked.

I knew what was in his heart as I saw his hand flex open and closed. I felt heartily sorry for him because this Mr. Darcy was so very much different. This one proved to have nice manners and was determined to make it easy on me this time; this one was eager to fall in love with me and there would be no fighting for his heart. And he really thought that he was making progress.

"I mean that I cannot do *this*," I said, stressing the last word. I was shutting him down. Rejecting him. Within the depths of my soul, I knew that I was not only thwarting our destiny, and the road that we must walk down, but also that I was hurting him. And, in many ways, I was hurting myself. I felt my love for him return, and how I was twisting my heart in two, willing to break myself to avoid suffering my fate. I knew that I was there to love him. That I was destined to always love him. Irrevocably and irresistibly. But I was choosing not to care.

"Why not?" he asked, understanding me.

"Because I can't," I said, my eyes filling with emotion. My

blood was boiling in my veins, my mind crying out that I was betraying myself—but I ignored it. "I just can't."

As I stood up to walk away and make a hasty retreat, Darcy turned to me sharply.

"Who was he?" he asked. "The man who hurt you. He really pulled a number on you, didn't he?"

I looked squarely at him, and I felt my expression burn into his eyes.

"He died. So, in a way, you can say he hurt me very much."

"Elizabeth—"

"Please. Let me walk away."

He shrunk back into his seat but didn't say anything.

I saw the pain in his eyes and did everything that I could to resist him.

"Thank you. Goodbye, Mr. Darcy."

"Goodbye, Elizabeth."

I nodded to him, slung my bag over my shoulder and raced away. Ignoring Clancy's look of concern, and Jenny, as she felt sorry for me, I dashed to the door and threw it open.

Once I was outside, the Rapture was building up within me.

Turn around, it cried. *Turn around and go back inside.*

The Rapture made my blood burn and I felt as if the sky was turning cloudy all because of my actions. My vision was becoming too sharp, and I could see things that were a mile away with perfect clarity. My smell was now inhaling everything, and it was burning my nose, and the sounds of traffic! A bus drove past me, and I had to cover my ears, or its sound would have made my eardrums burst. And the touch of the sidewalk was seeping through my shoes, and I felt it begin to pull my feet down.

To escape the rain, and to suppress the effects of the *Rapture,* I began to jog down the block. When I realized that the exercise was helping to suppress the symptoms, I quickened my pace.

The deafening sounds were lessening.

My sight was returning to normal.

The sidewalk was no longer pulling me down.

And quickly, I was no longer inhaling every scent that was in the air.

I ran faster.

Faster and faster.

I must have looked mad to all the people as I rushed past them, ran across the street just as a streetlight turned red, and told people to get out of the way.

When I was completely exhausted, I stopped, planted my hands on my knees, and began to gasp for air.

The *Rapture* was over.

I leaned against a bus sign, to rest and catch my breath better. Removing my heels from out of my flat shoes, I let my feet breathe.

Suddenly, there was a gunshot in the air.

The whole street was in chaos as a gunman raced out of a store, shooting into the crowd, and people began to run.

I stood there, transfixed, and not afraid of the event. In fact, blindly, I only felt compelled to move forward to the tragedy to find out if anyone was still alive and if I could suppress the attacker.

Despite my lack of stature, my experiences had given me surprising strength and I had experience at taking down mad gunmen before while ducking being shot at.

Therefore, I moved my way through the crowd that was rushing against me, and I felt like a fish trying to swim upstream.

From the people who were crying out for where their children were.

Women and men running away from the evil that they never thought would have happened to them.

The horror on their faces.

The devastation of possibly being innocent victims to some villain's evil.

The News would never show the innocent who died, but the villain who killed.

But I saw their faces as I rushed through the crowds that were pushing me backwards to escape being slaughtered.

I neared the shooter just as he shot another person. Taking a small bat out of my bag, and ducking behind a car that was behind him, I planned how I could throw the contents of my bag at him, distracting him as I would strike him across the face. I saw his victim fall on the ground.

It was a young man. Too young.

The scene of the crowd running. The gunman and the loss of life that fell before me.

And seeing Darcy again.

While I acted, it made me fall back into time. Back to when it all began…

CHAPTER 1

The Boston Massacre

March 5th, 1770

"Are we going in the right direction?" I cried as I followed Henry Lucas through the Boston streets.

"Yes!" he replied, turning swiftly around a corner at such a rate that it was hard for me to keep up with him. While I was somewhat fast at running, I had the misfortune to always be incumbered by clothes that did not lend itself to dashing up hill and down dale. Also, the cobbled streets, while safer for the carriage, coach, and cart, did not do for the shoes I wore, and I felt the weight of my burdens hanging about my limbs as exhaustion filled my spirits and I grew more winded.

Yet, the urgency of the hour, the desperation of the moment, and the acknowledgement of predetermining what might occur carried Mr. Lucas and me forward, as we headed to the town square.

"Oh, Collins!" I grunted, annoyed with what I might see when we arrived, "what have you gotten us into this time?"

"It's not just Collins, Lizzy," Mr. Lucas replied, his voice as harsh as mine from it being parched. "When I left them, there were many more ruffians falling upon the British soldier. Savages!"

I barely had time to swallow Henry Lucas's words as I had little time to consider how horrible this would all be for the cause that I pursued. What was savage to Henry was a humiliation for me.

"I feel as if I never should have come to Boston," I uttered to myself. Fortunately, it was low enough for Henry Lucas not to hear it, because I didn't want to offend him. After all, who in this world was not proud of where they were from? I am certain that I do not know. But ever since I had come to New England, I had been met with everything that I did not agree with when it pertained to what we were attempting to achieve.

From the burning of effigies—a habit I still blamed our mother country for teaching us that—to riots and violence against any loyalist whose shop could easily fall victim to mob rule—which I blamed all colonizing empires for—I felt shame.

As we grew closer to the square, and to King's Street, I heard raised voices. The sound grew deafening as the shouts rang out in the night air.

"Collins!" I hissed to myself. "Cousin, what have you done?"

When we turned a corner, the scene unfolded in front of us.

Houses, closed shops, and the curious looks of many people leaning their heads out of the window were behind us. And before us, King Street laid bare and ahead.

Suddenly, the grand unveiling rushed into view as we saw the Town House. Standing at its front were nine Redcoats, with their muskets aimed at a crowd of men shouting obscenities at the officers who were attempting to hold them at bay.

What made the scene even more horrible was the size of the

opposing force, the crowd of Bostonians and others who were so adversarial. The colonists who were shouting at the British officers were much greater in number, and the officers, who I looked upon, were not very old.

Except for two men who were at the head, shouting orders for their officers to steady as they yelled at the mob to disperse and return to their homes.

Our worst nightmare was presented to us.

"By god!" Henry cried, echoing the words that rang through my mind. "I never should have brought you here. Charlotte and my mother will never forgive me."

I stood there, horrified, as the event was not how Henry Lucas had described.

"I thought you said that a fight broke out between a private and an angry mob," I uttered, my voice hoarse, which was a natural result between being winded from running and from being speechless at what lay before me.

"Yes, it was," Mr. Lucas said, equally as astounded. "It's my friend, Private Hugh White. He's the soldier right there, nearest to the left."

I looked where he indicated, and I saw a young man with his musket aimed at the angry crowd. He had long blond hair that he kept tied in the back and his regimentals were as correctly put together as the rest. And like the rest, his face was uniform; in his eyes was panic, alarm, and resentment.

"When I left him," Henry elaborated, "Hugh was the only soldier guarding the King's money stored inside the Custom House. I went to speak to him, but then a set of angry men rushed toward him, insulting and threatening violence. White began to fight back, but look at him, Lizzy! He is just one man."

"He clearly got away."

"No," Henry said, "I did. Hugh struck a colonist with his bayonet, so the colonists pelted him with anything they could get their hands on. I managed to ring the nearest bells along the townhouse. I knew that would make them all disperse. It clearly did the opposite, and this is all my fault. As the crowd grew, I ran to get Captain Thomas Preston so that he could send more soldiers to help Hugh. While I was running to help, that was when I saw Collins in the crowd. I was hoping I could get you here in time to convince him to make the crowd disperse. You're the only person that he is afraid of."

"And we're too late," I said, my voice hollow as I felt so hopeless.

"Yes, we are. I was ignorant of it escalating this far. Elizabeth, come away, friend. I've brought you to danger."

I felt Henry place his hand on my arm, to take me away from anything that could happen next, but my feet were frozen to the spot.

My eyes could not rest anywhere but on the sight before me. For, indeed, that is the reality of horrible images: they are the most provocative thing to one's inner peace. And yet, we cannot tear our eyes away from the scene that lies before us.

That was me now.

I ought to leave. It was logical for me to leave. But there I would remain, and once more, the instinct—or rather the frightful gift of foresight—found me and I knew what was about to happen.

Then, I rested my eyes on the British soldiers who the mob was harassing.

The mob were fools! Why couldn't the colonists see what

they were doing? Destroying every wise notion, all justification that we had for our revolutions! I hated them.

And then my eyes rested on one of the British leaders. One was Captain Thomas Preston, but my eyes immediately fell to the other man. He was a man, so wholly like many others.

But a mist seemed to fall upon my vision, and I felt a haziness. It fell heavily upon my present judgments, and for a moment, I wholly forgot the events that surrounded me. The whole world fell away as I felt my blood run hot and cold all at once. The ground beneath my feet seemed to connect to me and take a strong hold on me. The wind whipped around my head, making my mobcap fall off and my blonde hair began to become untied, falling down my face and whipping along my cheeks.

I did not watch, but merely saw my cap soar through the air, away from me.

It glided along the winds, over the crowd and seemed to have a mind of its own as it soared toward the British troops and fell at the feet of the man who I had watched.

His height was taller than what was usual, his figure striking, his countenance elegant, and his face had something of a keen look. His expression was intelligent and had all the appearance of a man who had a quickness of mind.

Suddenly, I grew afraid of him. For my eyes could not leave him, and I found it most disagreeable to be so easily taken away.

I wanted to turn around and run away from the man, in hopes of being free from an invisible spell that brought me to the place where I now was.

And the white of my cap along with the chaos that it clashed against did not escape this officer. When he saw the cap, he looked down at it, and his eyes searched frantically, worried that there was a woman present.

As his eyes moved past the crowd, they suddenly rested on me.

We were far from each other. He never should have known me, seen me, or taken heed of me. As I ought not to see him.

And yet, the space between us drew suddenly close. His expression seemed to shorten the gap and I saw his face as near as Henry Lucas's was to me.

The wind picked up, swerved around my feet once more, the spark of life ignited in me, and I felt a connection. Then I saw his eyes, and it was unlike anything I had ever seen.

His eyes said nothing, but I knew better.

He was heartbroken and afraid. The colonists were attacking him and his fellow officers. He was astonished but refused to show it. So, how did I know?

Who was this man? What was he thinking?

"Darcy!" Captain Thomas Preston cried, shaking Darcy's shoulder. "What are you thinking, man?" Hearing his name had brought Darcy back to the present altercation that he was facing. But the return was slow and agonizing.

For, whether by his power or not, he had not been there. His body had been behind the officers, but his mind, soul and spirit had been transported across the town square, away from the Town House, and rested at the feet of a strange woman. At first, it was as if the gruesome scene that he was amidst had quite faded away from his consciousness. And all the horrors that were before him had fallen and a great curtain of calmness had rested over him as his focus had gone adrift, to the unknown lady.

She was far away, and yet, her figure felt close, as his body rushed into a series of hot and cold, of peace and activity, and all sound had faded into a gentle hum into his ears.

But when Captain Preston's voice rung true, he was driven out of his distractions, and he returned to the scene at hand.

At last, Darcy tore his eyes from the lady, and it was as if the reality had rushed back to him, to such a degree, that it almost made him fall.

The immense crowd of rabblerousers overpowered his vision.

Their obscene shouts almost rendered him deaf.

And the pounding of their feet against the ground made the earth beneath them shake.

And all the while, he and Captain Preston had nine young British officers in their defense.

Where there were no colonists, suddenly, there had been a crowd. And where there had been a small crowd, it had become a violent mob.

"Where is your head, man?" Preston repeated.

"Forgive me, Captain," Darcy apologized, returning to his noble and professional stature. "There was a woman in the back. I worried for her safety."

"If she is here, then that is not your responsibility," Preston responded, shouting over the mob's noise. "Whoever she is, she is of no consequence."

Instinctively, Darcy felt offense at this suggestion. Suddenly, within his breasts, he felt an immediate concern and compassion for the strange woman who was on the streets so late in the evening. For what was a lady doing up and about at that time of night?

Then he was struck by a stick that the Bostonians had thrown at him. This was enough for him to remember himself.

"Aye, Captain," Darcy said, raising his musket and moving to the other side of their small force. As he looked out into the braggards who were harassing the men who were guarding the townhouse, he had become both angry as well as horrified.

They are attacking us, he thought to himself. *Our colonists are really attacking us. I cannot fathom, nor can dissemble— they hate us. Truly, they hate the very idea of us.*

This discovery had no choice but to affect his heart, even though he did not show it, in any fashion. From the outside, he appeared to be as hard looking as ever, his jaw set, his scowl a permanent fixture on his face.

"Lieutenant," one of the officers whispered nearby.

Darcy turned his head and faced the young man. In the young man's eyes was terror, panic, and anxiety. Even worse, it was apparent that the man was on the verge of crying.

"Will we die today, sir?" the young man questioned, about to begin weeping.

Within his heart, Darcy empathized and cried out to the man. However, it was not his place to show it. He was a lieutenant; it was *never* his place to show it.

"Whatever happens," Darcy uttered, "it is not our place to show any fear."

When hearing that, the officer's face blanched, his weeping dissolved and the familiar instinct—the instinct to be a man— had taken full effect. His moment of weakness would be eventually looked upon as an act of cowardice and sentiment. What was the young man to do but suppress any of these fears and be willing to lay down his life, for a future that he was not allowed to have? And never allowed to see.

Darcy moved along the edge of Captain Preston's small unit of soldiers and appealed to the colonists.

"This assembly and gathering is unlawful and dictatorial!" Darcy bellowed. "Disperse and go back to your homes."

However, the mob only continued to berate and torment the

regulars. And Darcy saw out of the side of his eye, the officers were fearing for their lives.

Suddenly, with no knowledge of where the shouts were coming from, a cry rang out into the night.

"Fire!"

~

"Fire!"

That word penetrated my attention, and I was torn from my focus on the British lieutenant, and the word brought me back out of the cloud that I had fallen into.

"No!" I cried.

And just as the word was declared, my vision became more direct, and among the rabblerousers, I saw my cousin, William Collins. He had been among the middle of the Bostonians, and next to him were two men who I was also familiar with: George Hughes, a Boston shoemaker, and a friend of mine, the freeman Crispus Attucks.

"By god!" I whispered under my breath as I saw the shock on their faces as the word also rang in their ears. Their faces went from anger to alarm as that was the sound—the horrible sound that brought tragedy and defined the road that we would all walk down.

Gunshots began to fill the air.

The redcoats fired into the violent crowd.

Despite the smoke that rose in the air, I not only saw the entire spectacle, but I also could practically taste the moods, the devastation, and the tragedy as it hung about the street, displayed before my very eyes. The feeling was within me. The sensation of being part of it all. Every moment, every soldier, everyone in the crowd—it was as if I was complete with them, as if I connected with every element of their beings. I was within the massacre, while not being a part of it at all, and looking down on it from where I stood.

As I saw men scurry away from the onslaught, I felt their panic.

I could sense the desperation and the horror in the redcoats' eyes as they continued to fire at the mob.

For every colonist who fell, I felt a pang in my stomach of their lives leaving.

I crouched down on the ground, clutching my chest and trying to collect myself. Seeing me fall on the cobblestones, Henry must've assumed that I was devastated by the scene before me.

He crouched down and, forgetting himself, wrapped his arms around me to carry me away.

"Eliza, we need to leave," he declared.

"I can't leave," I whispered, winded. For reasons that I was unaware of, I had to stay. I was too drawn to the scene. Too much a part of it, despite that it had nothing to do with me. It was something that I could not explain, and if I had tried, Henry Lucas would have thought that I was going mad.

"You must," Henry said. "This is no place for a lady."

"I am no lady," I replied, my voice hoarse as I felt the pain of a British officer firing into the crowd, and the agony of a Bostonian falling to the ground. "I must stay. Help me stand, please," I uttered as I tried to get to my knees.

Mr. Lucas tried, but with each attempt, my knees buckled under another gunshot. This was not fear or devastation. I was feeling the weight of something else.

The weight of *someone* else.

And then there it was again: the link.

I raised my eyes and glimpsed the Redcoats. Firing into the crowd, I saw the man who I had been staring at before, with his musket raised.

When seeing him again, I only felt the weight on me worsen. As if I were being hurled down to an abyss. I knew that this sensation was not coming from within me, but from without. I could not fathom, but I felt a binding tie. As if my broken spirits were not coming from myself, but from elsewhere.

While assisting his soldiers, Darcy did not falter as he felt his emotions cause such a drain from him. It was as if it were a grand release and his anxiety, his woes, his heartache, his anger was all dripping outside of his body and drifting off, to an invisible force.

For a moment, he wondered if it was God.

But while this was spiritual in origin, it felt less like the holistic and more like the mundane—the corporeal. He could not fathom why, but he felt as if his emotions were being absorbed...by someone else.

As the smoke from the muskets filled the air, and the cries filled the street, along with the pounding of scurrying feet that were rushing from the volleys of Captain Preston's officers, Darcy wanted to cry.

He could see nothing. But he felt everything. He felt the agony of the men who had to fire into the crowd.

He felt the anger of the mob.

And his mind linked with those who fell to the ground, never to wake again.

But the woman! Where was the woman? She was too far to have received a blow. But not far enough that she could have been trampled over by a throng running for their very lives. People have died in stampedes, both human and animal. In the streets of Boston, anything could happen.

Curse the smoke that clouded his vision.

~

Curse the smoke that made it hard for me to see the reward for the mob's cruel behavior. Were these actions of patriotism? Is this what we had come to?

Finding my strength, I moved away from Henry Lucas, who had remained on the ground. Out of the side of my eye, I saw as he tried to follow me, insisting that I come away. Refusing, I kept moving forward.

"The redcoats have emptied their muskets," I said, my voice distant, as if I was in a daze. "I know an empty barrel when I hear one. We are out of danger."

"That does not signify that the hazards are over," he insisted.

"I must find Collins and see if he is alive. And Crispus. I must ensure that Crispus and George Hughes are alive."

Releasing myself from Henry's hold on my arm, I lifted my petticoats and raced toward the unfortunate event.

"Elizabeth!" Henry cried, running after me. Despite that I was wearing heavier garments, he was never a constant runner, so he could not reach me as I dashed onward.

Rushing toward the confusion, and the smoke that filled my vision, soon the scene cleared, and I stopped in my tracks.

There were men on the ground, injured, and rolling over. Some were moaning as they were trampled over, others had been shot, and some just were too stunned to move.

But I had a mission, and I did not have time to care for them. After all, in their passions or drunkenness, they had chosen to walk into this calamity, with their eyes opened, and not as the actions of intelligent individuals, but as one blind and brash collective.

Moving around the men, I called out.

"William!" I cried. "Crispus! George Hughes!"

"Elizabeth!" I heard my name. It belonged to my cousin, Sons of Liberty member, William Collins. "Over here!"

I raced through the smoky air, to where I heard the voice, stumbling over a few wounded men in the process, and eventually, I saw my cousin's familiar figure through the haze.

"William!" I cried, running to him. I knelt on the ground next to him, seeing that his arm was bleeding.

"They fired on us," he cried as I tore open his smock and inspected the wound.

"What did you expect!" I asked, removing some bandages from my satchel, as well as removing some aloe plant ointment and some ale. "William, tell me that you did not cause this."

William looked at me, the pain ruining any chance of trying to appear intimidating.

"Don't tell me that you helped collect this mob?" I asked, pouring the ale on the wound, placing the aloe paste on the laceration and wrapping the plaster around it, to keep it closed. "The bullet went straight through. Gangrene should not set in. And—"

I looked past him and saw George Hughes further along, crouched down on the ground, holding a man. I recognized his outline, and it made my blood turn cold.

"Crispus," I uttered, horrified. Moving past Collins, I walked over to George Hughes, leaned down and beheld the corpse that he was holding. I rolled the man's face over and saw that it was Crispus Attucks.

"Oh no," I whispered. Seeing the devastation in my eyes, George Hughes was mortified.

"I'm sorry, Lizzy," George whispered to me. "We never should have encouraged him to join us."

"It's not your fault," I said, beginning to weep as I placed my hand over Crispus's heart and made certain that he was dead. "I knew that this would happen again. He ran away to be free, and now this is it? It's not fair. It's not fair at all."

Crispus Attucks, a dear friend of mine, was gone.

From above me, I sensed Henry Lucas as he leaned down and pat my shoulder to offer me solace.

Instinctively, I took George Hughes's place and held Crispus Attucks in my arms.

Looking down on him, I saw his eyes wide open, despite that the life had left him. Feeling sorry for the man who had escaped to freedom, only to leave life this way, made me wonder how fruitless everything seemed to be.

Suddenly, I felt the euphoria envelop me again.

Tearing my eyes away from my friend's corpse, I looked toward the British lines.

Behind the nine soldiers, I saw Captain Preston talking with the man who had captured my attention. His tall and noble posture both enraptured me and antagonized me. I felt drawn to him, and I didn't like it.

~

From behind his soldiers, as Captain Preston was giving his orders, and he was tending to the officers to see if anyone was wounded, Darcy felt the strange woman's gaze on him.

Unable to resist, he turned and looked at her, and found her eyes set on him. Their gazes locked, and he knew. Without understanding why but he knew.

He felt drawn to her, and he *didn't* like it.

He saw her leaning over one of the dead men in the crowd, a Negro man—what an absurd thing for a lady to be doing. When seeing the look in her eye, he also was aware of something else:

She was a rebel.

~

When looking into his eyes, I knew what this lieutenant was thinking: he knew that I was a patriot.

And he was my enemy.

~

'She is my enemy,' Darcy realized. There was something about her countenance that enticed him, but also gave off the feeling of defiance. How could he know such a thing? He had never met the lady, but still, his instincts were too driven.

And they were correct.

~

"And I am his enemy," I said to myself as the English lieutenant stared at me. "And he knows it. He has no right to know what is in my heart. No right at all! How dare he."

But in my eyes was a burning defiance, and I was wholly aware of it. He must have felt the heat of my anger, as I sensed the heat of his despair.

I think he knew it.

That this was just the beginning between the British empire and her American colonies.

This is the beginning of a crisis.

We cannot go back to the way that we were.

~

"I cannot fathom it," Captain Preston declared, equally as horrified and enraged at the scenario that lay before him, as Darcy had been. "Our own colonists attacked us."

"We had no choice, Captain," Darcy said, still staring at the woman who intrigued him.

"This is deplorable."

"Worse, sir. This is the beginning of the crisis. We cannot go back to the way we were. Our colonies are against us."

Lieutenant Fitzwilliam Darcy knew.

This was the beginning of a parting of the ways. It was the beginning of Britain losing its colonies.

I knew.

This was the beginning of a parting of the ways.

Mother England has lost us as its colonies.

CHAPTER 2
Four Years Later...

I t's a reality, no matter how much you prepare yourself, there is always anxiety of when you return to a place where so much tragedy had occurred.

In the four years that I had been away from Massachusetts, I had grown to be wary of the place. From all the news that had reached Philadelphia, the New England crisis had not only increased, but had risen to a passionate momentum.

Before the Boston Massacre had occurred, there were already over two thousand British soldiers patrolling the Boston streets, to enforce taxation. The immediate response was riots, rebellions, violence, and destruction of property on both sides. The whole place had become a powder keg of disaster, with the massacre being enough to have driven me out of the Massachusetts colony entirely. But one ought to 'never say *never'*.

Sitting in the post wagon, I was filled with both excitement and dread as we pulled into the outskirts of Boston.

"Get ready for it, lass!" the postman, a Welshman named Lugeon, said as he turned around a collection of trees.

Originally, I had been sitting in the back of the wagon, along with all the haversacks of mail. The cold had become overpowering, so I had been wrapped in blankets, using the mailbags as more insulation as I folded them around me. Therefore, when Lugeon announced our arrival, I scurried from out of my warm place—regretting losing the hot space immediately—dashed through the wagon and went to the box seat next to Lugeon as he steered his horses.

As I plopped down next to him, Lugeon couldn't help but laugh at my lack of grace.

"Aye," I acknowledged, "I abandoned trying to be graceful a long time ago. I left that talent to my sisters."

"Beggin' your pardon, but I'm not complaining, lass," Lugeon responded. "I like it."

"Of course, you do," I said. "I do not think that I would respect you if you did not see my own sort of charm."

Smiling, I looked out to see the vastness of the city, the work of civilization, and I marveled at the landscape before me.

Being one of the few cities to rival Philadelphia with its structure, Boston had beautiful brick buildings, cobble-paved roads, many taverns—the Green Dragon being the main one that I had previously gone to—the port had many ships that made berth there, and I was able to see urbanization laid out before me, after spending so many days traveling through rural countryside and provincial towns.

"I thought you said that you were dreading coming back to this city," Lugeon remarked, slowing his horses to a halt so that they could rest, and he could get them some water from a stream that was to our left.

"I was and I am," I said, "but my courage has a way of rising with every attempt to intimidate me. Besides, this scene is better than what I imagined."

"What did you imagine?" Lugeon asked as he went down to the stream with a bucket he took from his cart.

"Chaos," I admitted, "after all, it's been only three months since the Sons of Liberty dumped the tea into the harbor. I was worried of being met with British Regulars marching through the streets, houses being on fire, and—I think I imagined the worst."

I jumped down and began to pat one of the horses along its mane.

"That is the one benefit to imagining the worst of outcomes; everything has no choice but to be above your expectations. Now, I can smile."

"Sons of liberty," Lugeon spat. "Sons of the Devil, more like."

As I had ridden with Lugeon, I had gathered a knowledge of the man that he was.

Lugeon was no patriot.

But he was not a loyalist either.

He was just indifferent to it all.

He was against the Stamp Act and the Townshend Act when it was released.

But he also had no desire to be at odds with our mother country.

He did not like the idea of the oppressive taxation and we colonists having no say in anything. He was also upset that our years of peacefully attempting to gain those rights had been denied.

But he was against the resort to violence that the Sons of Liberty had taken to achieve their ends and goals at protests.

I never despised Lugeon because while I did not agree with his indifferent side, I did agree with his concerns. Besides, he was harmless, and never was the sort to repeat our arguments with others that passed our way. I knew that he would never report me to any authorities, just because of my liberal tongue and speech.

"With that, we do agree at least," I accepted.

"Ah, you agree with me?" Lugeon said as he put the water to his horse's mouth, and it drank. "That's the third time that we agreed on something since I took you on as baggage."

"Call me baggage one more time, Lugeon, and I'll tell you where you can stuff all these letters," I retorted.

Lugeon laughed.

"We Welsh like a girl with spirit, so I have no choice, do I?"

"No, Lugeon, you don't. It's too much a part of your nature."

"Yeah, I reckon it might be."

He went down to the stream again to get water for his second horse.

As I rubbed the second horse's back, I continued to look out over Boston.

"Your friend must think really high of herself to have you come to her wedding during these times," Lugeon said over his shoulder. "Because mark my words, lass. The trouble is coming soon again."

"It's Boston; there's always trouble. Besides, Charlotte Lucas is worth it. I would never forgive myself if I missed it. For a time, she never favored the idea of marriage, so her fiancé is very special. I wouldn't miss this for the world—even if the world is on fire. Besides, she couldn't help that those men would raid a ship and dump all that tea overboard. Her happy event just came at a moment of terrible timing. Right event at the wrong era, I daresay."

"And one mustn't hide from the world?" Lugeon pointed out as he gave the water to the second horse.

"No, one must not do that," I agreed, then I smelled myself. "Oh, dear lord! I smell horrible!"

Lugeon laughed again. I slapped his shoulder.

"What?" He called after me as I rushed down to the stream,

taking out some lye soap that I had acquired on the road. "You did not foresee that?"

"I blame you," I called behind him as I removed my stockings and shoes and unfastened my short gown. "Your odor has drifted down to me."

"No, it did not," he protested. Then he smelled himself and changed his tune. "Oh, my mistake. You did get it from me."

"You're a bad habit, Lugeon, just by being in your presence."

Lugeon chuckled again.

Despite the cold, I still washed down parts of my person, while still remaining fully clothed. I had ordered Lugeon to look away as I sponge-bathed, he was kind enough to oblige, and then we proceeded to go into the city.

As we rolled through the streets, I began to see familiar spots that I had visited before, when I had last come to Boston, four years ago.

That was the road that I had run down when Charlotte and I had to rush to morning meeting.

Lugeon rolled into the marketplace, and we passed a few British officers who were patrolling the streets.

I had to avert my gaze, so as not to look on them. Boston was still being occupied. Boston was *always* being occupied since I could remember.

Then we pulled into the main square, where the Town House had been.

And the memory of the Boston Massacre had come rushing back to me, as if it had been yesterday.

The madness, the horror, the savagery, and the lives that were lost there.

And the lieutenant in the regulars.

Suddenly, I felt the pang in my stomach again. My smile disappeared and I grabbed at my waist.

I had not felt that sensation in four years. And it was emerging again. At first, I attributed this unease to the memory of the incident, but I was of the suspicion that it was something else.

I felt as if something had just entered Boston.

Or someone.

∼

"Drop anchor!" Admiral Bernick cried as the Dauntless arrived at the Boston harbor.

Emerging from his cabin, Captain Fitzwilliam Darcy climbed on deck, walked to the ship's railing, and leaned out over it.

With a heavy heart, he beheld the city before him. Despite that it had been years since he had seen the place, Boston and Massachusetts seemed to be much as it ever was: a place where he loved to look on, but had no desire to step into ever again.

As the anchor was dropped into the water, Darcy breathed in deeply and was determined to do his duty. Therefore, against his internal wishes, he was the first to get in the rowboats and row ashore, to Boston harbor.

As he neared land, he felt a heaviness in him. What he did was for King and country—and for the Darcy pride. Although, deep within, he was anxious. He had a premonition; Boston would be his undoing.

The rowboat reached the docks, and as Darcy disembarked, standing on the Boston shore, his legs buckled and felt as if they were collapsing on him.

He clutched his stomach and had to keep from stumbling.

"Captain," a regular said behind him, concerned for his superior's welfare, "are you well? You look ill."

And ill was how he felt.

The second that he had stepped onto the city's land, an old ailment had seized him. It was the weight of his spirit being drained from him, while his lifeforce also temporarily escaped.

He felt as if his soul had reached out, found an outside element, and wrapped itself around it.

He had not felt that sensation in… four years.

Assuming that it was the fear of what lay ahead, he attributed it all down to nerves.

"I am well," Darcy said to the officer. "Thank you, Private."

Immediately recovering, Darcy shook off the effects and walked along the docks, where his escort was waiting to take him to the British headquarters.

Wholly unaware he was that his affliction had been the reaction of his senses being linked to an arrival.

For it would only be a matter of time before he realized that, at the precise time he had come to Boston, a woman had done so as well.

And she would be his undoing.

The greatest undoing of all.

CHAPTER 3
Greetings

We arrived at one of the local posts in the city, where Lugeon had parked his wagon at the front, next to a set of horses that I could tell were used for dispatch.

Just as he arrived, two middle-aged men emerged, rolling down their shirtsleeves and putting on their jackets.

"Lugeon," one of them said, "perfect timing, man."

"Did you already sort out the mail?" another man asked him, getting into the wagon.

"Aye, I did well enough," Lugeon responded, "but you lads need to check again, and send out when you confirmed. You can't go riding off just yet."

"We have to be quicker, now more than ever. The British brutes are beginning to intercept letters. Things have changed since you've been gone."

"Things always change when I am gone," Lugeon grunted. "And by the way, did you learn your manners in a barn, the lot of you? Neither of you greeted the lady with me. By zounds! Chivalry, lads!"

Indeed, they had treated me as if I had been invisible. I was not surprised by this. Between my plain dress, and my meek appearance, I must not have looked like anything particular to them. But still!

"Thank you, Lugeon." I was grateful.

The two men remembered themselves, removed their hats, and nodded to me.

"Miss," the first one said.

"Miss," the second one said.

"Bennet," I replied, "Miss Elizabeth Bennet. A pleasure to make your acquaintance."

"The pleasure will be short-lived," Lugeon responded.

"Oi!" the second man said, "we can be friendly."

"Is disregarding me as you being kind?" I asked, unafraid to retaliate.

Both men were a little humbled by this. I liked that; it showed that they were not filled with self-importance and could be self-aware.

"Beggin' your pardon, Miss Bennet," one of the men said, and then his eyes lit up when he recalled something. "Oh, you must be the lady that the gentleman inside is waiting for."

My spirits became elated when I knew that I was going to be escorted to Lucas Lodge. After all, it was a long walk there from the post office.

"It must be Henry Lucas," I said, going into the wagon and taking out my luggage and pistols. When the men saw the weapons were mine, their eyes widened in shock. I put all my items in my haversack and Lugeon helped lug it out of the wagon, putting it on the ground.

I rushed into the office.

"Henry!" I cried when I saw the back of a man. When he turned around, he smiled, and I frowned.

It was not Henry Lucas.

It was my cousin, William Collins.

~

When seeing my changed expression, Collins's eyes drooped.

"Ah," he said, "that's not happiness to see me, I gather."

"Collins," I sighed.

"And after I was the one who eagerly came to greet you and deliver you to Lucas Lodge."

I groaned inwardly.

"I am grateful for that."

Collins raised an eyebrow.

"You don't look it."

"I cannot help it, Will."

"I know. It's your habit."

I grimaced.

"And what do you mean by my *habit*?"

William clapped his hands. He always did that when he wanted to delay an unpleasant conversation.

"Cousin, the Lucases are excited to see you once more, and it would be best to convey you to their residence."

"Yes," I replied, smoothly, using an analogy to indicate that this was a conversation for another time and another place, "after all, one must not wash one's dirty linens in the street, must one?"

My cousin was a fool in one way, but a shrewd and intelligent person in another way. He was a fool when it came to protests and romance, but a genius when it came to being deductive.

"It's talk like that which got you written out of the Quaker Meeting," he observed.

"Dirty linens," I reminded him, with a hint of malice in my voice. "Dirty linens, cousin."

"Quite right," he said, willing to comply. It made me smile. Despite his eager acts in protests and riots, William Collins was still afraid of me. I would always take advantage of that. "Well, let us be off then."

I bid good day to the two postmen and as my cousin put my luggage on the back of his horse and climbed onto the saddle, I turned to Lugeon.

"I have the painful feeling that we may never meet again," I commented.

"Boston is a big place," Lugeon responded. "But other times, it can also be quite small."

I raised an eyebrow, showing him that I saw through his wit.

"I panicked," he rushed out. "I actually don't know what I meant by that. I just didn't know what to say."

"I know you didn't know," I replied, amused. "But *I do* know what you meant."

"Curious little snip you are."

"Yes, I very much am."

Collins gave me his hand to help me up. I took it and wrapped my hands around his waist, riding behind him in sidesaddle.

"Till the next time or not!" I called to Lugeon.

"Right you are there!" Lugeon replied, waving as I rode away from him.

Despite the busyness on the streets, William and I were still able to talk and hear each other well.

"What did you mean back there?" I asked him.

"What did I mean back when?" he pointed out.

"When you said that it was my habit," I responded, "what did you mean by that?"

"You tend to have an implacable sort of resentment. Lizzy,

when you get upset with someone, it takes a long time for you to forgive them."

"Will," I responded, "I thank you for retrieving me, but can't you understand why I am still upset?"

"It was four years ago!"

"And nine men died from it. You helped start the Boston Massacre that attacked British officers, and it led to our friends dying."

"You think that I don't know that?" He retorted. "You think that I did not feel any sort of guilt when seeing that Crispus and the rest were dead?"

I squinted, surprised that he showed any sort of remorse on the tragedy.

"You never mentioned it," I retorted. "You never once apologized for helping gather that mob who stormed the townhouse."

"At the time, it was hard for me to apologize," William responded. "Try knowing that you gathered a force that led to your friends dying. I have had to live with that, and I had no choice but to come to terms with this revelation. But there is something that you are forgetting, Lizzy?"

"What?"

"That I am an influential man, but I do not have the power to order men's lives. All those men who stood with me did it of their own choosing. I am not the only one to blame, because each man's soul is his own. The men who died, their lives are not on my conscience anymore. Because they chose to be a part of our cause."

Inwardly, I was angry. Yes, he helped stir up the colonists, but he was also correct. Each man chose to be a part of that crowd. They made the choice. Whether I liked it or not, they were responsible for their own actions.

"I acknowledge," I gave way, "that you are partly correct.

You are not to blame for them being there. But Will, you know that people follow you, and with that weight, comes responsibility."

"You insult me, but you also flatter me."

"That's the sort of cousin that I am. But since this new crisis—"

"Ah, you heard about the tea being thrown overboard the Dartmouth?"

I rolled my eyes.

"Cousin, don't insult me. Anyone who can read, or has ears, knows about that. You were there, were you not?"

"Yes," he admitted, "I was among the party that took part in our patriotism. The Tea Act was unlawful and deserved an equally unlawful response. Are you about to tell me that I behaved badly?"

"Not particularly. I do not deny the idea of protest, especially since I heard that you all were insistent on not damaging private property. But won't the Boston people suffer for your actions?"

"They already are. Our informants have sent private word that the British are not only sending more reinforcements, but they are considering enforcing even greater curfews on Boston."

My eyes widened at the repercussions of this act of radicalism.

"King George would really undertake that?"

You are surprised by the same man who does not understand taxation without presentation? He does not care about us. And Prime Minister, Lord North, is the worst. But all that matters is what money that they can bleed from out of us. Even now, we still get no say in matters and have no voice. We tried to settle things peacefully, for years, and we went ignored. Only more soldiers were sent to suppress the problem."

"But do you worry over the future?"

"Of course, I do. But I know that this is the correct thing. It shows the king and parliament that we will not disappear and that we act as we speak: as courageous men." He tore his eyes from the road. "Lizzy, you and I disagree on many things, but you are not a coward either. You know what I speak is true. And I daresay that you understand me. Or am I wrong? Are you not a patriot?"

"Never consider me as anything but," I stated simply, but strongly. "But be prepared, cousin. You have woken a viper. Be prepared for that."

"Oh, we will be. I can assure you. We will be."

We rode on, going down State Street. It was a financial district, and as we rode past the Old State House and the Boston Custom House, there were some broadsides pasted against some walls, showing protests that were being torn down by watchmen who must've been hired by the Massachusetts governor.

"We live in strange times," William noted.

"That's just what the generations before us said," I noted. "The times are always strange. We just stumbled upon it after society began to have a defined sense of what normal was."

Eventually, we pulled into the neighborhood, Boston Proper, and we drove along Beacon Hill, and eventually arrived at the North End.

As we turned down another street, I smiled when I fell upon a familiar sight.

"Lucas Lodge," I cried.

"Yes," Mr. Collins replied, not as elated as I was. I think he never really forgave the Lucases for remaining loyal to King George and Britain. "Welcome back to Lucas Lodge, Lizzy."

CHAPTER 4

Darcy Takes Command

When his carriage arrived at the Town House on King's Street, Darcy could not help but fall back into the recesses of his memories. His mind dashed back over the years, in 1770, when he and Captain Preston had to fend off the Bostonians who attacked them.

And then, his thoughts flew back to when he, Preston and the officers had to stand on trial, having been accused of murdering colonists. The weight of being falsely accused was like that of a heavy blanket of torture, or like that of a meta-physical iron maiden that was galvanizing him.

He was certain of his innocence and that of his soldiers. But the anxiety of it, of being in the courtroom, awaiting a verdict that he was not certain on which way that he would fall.

Therefore, when he was declared innocent, he finally felt the weight lift, but not as if the crisis had ended.

Now, he was sent back, and the oppressive feeling had returned to his chest. But still, he was a younger son who also had a profound sense of duty. When the orders were given, and his Majesty had ordered Darcy back to the colonies, who was he to refuse?

Eventually, they arrived at the Hutchinson House, the grand estate that belonged to Massachusetts governor Thomas Hutchinson, the carriage parked, and Darcy was admitted.

Due to the dangers and threats that the rebel ruffians had exerted to the Governor when he refused to repeal the Tea Act, the British generals used his home as their residency, more so for the task of protecting the Governor, rather than out of their own convenience.

Once Darcy was admitted into the house, he was asked to wait in the parlor, until Colonel Forster's Sergeant informed Darcy that the Colonel would see him now.

With his papers and orders in his hand, Darcy went into the study, and was met by Colonel Forster poring over some maps and papers, with a sextet and pen in his hand.

"Captain Fitzwilliam Darcy," Darcy said with his strong voice, standing at attention and giving a salute. "Reporting for duty."

"Yes, yes, yes," Colonel Forster replied, still looking over the map and not looking at Darcy. "Your letter was received. I must say that you are one of the few officers who was expert at timing his arrival to the letter." Still not looking at Darcy, Colonel Forster removed a letter from under the other papers, showing that it was Darcy's estimated time of arrival.

"I prefer to be precise," Darcy responded, still standing at attention. "Colonel Forster, I brought my papers and orders."

"At ease, Captain. And place your orders on the table."

Darcy did so, and Colonel Forster took the orders and looked them over.

"Your reputation proceeds you, Captain. I congratulate you on your recent promotion."

"Thank you, sir."

At last, Colonel Forster turned to Darcy. Seeing his posture, Colonel Forster raised an eyebrow.

"Captain, I said you could stand at ease."

"Sir, I am at ease."

Colonel Forster chuckled, amazed that this captain's idea of being 'at ease', was the same as when he was standing at attention: tall, intense, strict, and solemn.

In a moment, Forster knew the nature of the man he'd recently met.

~

Refreshment was ordered, and Colonel Forster took a seat while Darcy respectfully still stood.

"Welcome back to Boston," Colonel Forster began.

"With respect, sir," Darcy said, stoically, "I doubt that Massachusetts will welcome me."

"Too right," Colonel Forster said, still analyzing this young man who was intent on being serious—almost too serious. "I heard rumors, Captain, that when you were given orders to return to New England, you secretly were disgruntled with your command."

"If I grumbled, I can assure you that I did not do it to my superiors."

"I am aware. But you are in a safe place here, lad, and are not here to be judged. I can very well understand that you were apprehensive about returning. Your last experience here proved to be unpleasant."

"Permission to speak freely."

"Permission granted."

"Unpleasant is a euphemism for what I went through. The Bostonians wanted us to be lined up against a wall and shot, stirred on by the fictitious drawings that the vicious Paul Revere posted in the papers. If it weren't for attorney John

Adams arguing that we acted in self-defense, I would have been dragged out to face the mob."

"I'm certain it would not have come to that."

"Colonel, I was there. That's what they wanted. They would have been happy if I were executed. Not many of these rebels are like John Adams, where they flatter themselves to be revolutionary, but they still are impartial."

"That's another problem; the Adams family. John Adams may be considered obnoxious and irrational at times, but he is fair. Unlike his cousin, Samuel Adams, who is nothing short of being the worst man in Boston. Yes. Some of our best spies are constantly keeping watch on Samuel Adams."

"And you have no choice but to. He is dangerous, sir."

"He has already proven so. Our intelligence had discovered that he was the main perpetrator who organized the 'Tea Party' and had led the mob going onboard the Dartmouth, the Eleanor, and the Beaver, and dumping 342 pounds of tea overboard. We lost the equivalent of 18,000 pounds."

Despite that Darcy was a man prone to giving few gestures, he scratched his chin and rubbed his mouth. This was the sort of world that he was returning to. Since he had lived in Massachusetts for almost two years following the aftermath of the Stamp Act and Townshend Act, he was there when uprisings first began in Boston. The main thing that he knew was going to be one of the most trying times of his life.

"You are aware of your duties and what you were summoned from England to uphold."

"I do, Colonel. Due to my experience with the Bostonian uprisings, I was promoted to assist my superiors when the Coercive Acts become official. Once all is arranged, we will implement the closing of Boston harbor to merchant shipping, establish formal British military rule in Massachusetts, and shall stress the Quartering Act."

"Very good. This will not be easy, and I warn you that you will be met with opposition. But we will succeed at showing these repulsive rebels that his Majesty's military will not suffer traitors to pass."

"Colonel, with respect, I can guarantee that we have set our intent on disbanding the Sons of Liberty. However, it will be neither easy nor wholly possible. Four years ago, I was still stationed here, and I saw it with my own eyes. They are dangerous, but they also are not likely to go quietly into the night."

"But your job will be to assist in making it so," Colonel Forster pressed.

Darcy did not see the realism to this. While he despised the Sons of Liberty better than any proper British captain, he still knew his adversary—perhaps even better than they knew themselves. After the Boston Tea Party, they were not going to stop there. They were regrouping. Mark his words and his thoughts.

"Aye, sir." Darcy stood even more erect.

When seeing this strong man willing to relent, Colonel Forster was able to relax a little around him, but not too much.

"Captain, I am not the usual man to inquire too much for a man's position in life, but you were raised on Pemberley, in Derbyshire."

"Yes, I was. When my father passed away a few years ago, my older brother took ahold of the estate, as the rightful heir."

"I've heard that it is one of the loveliest homes in England."

When hearing praise of his home, Darcy's eyes softened for a second, before he returned to his professional scowl. Whenever Pemberley received compliments, it always appealed to his softer side, for Darcy always felt that he was at his best whenever he was at home.

"Thank you, sir," Darcy responded. "I do not mean to speak from improper pride, but Pemberley is truly the best place on earth."

"From the prestige that would proceed from that, and the high rank that you are descended from, as well as if mingled with the service you rendered in New England when the Townshend Acts occurred, might I ask why it took you so long to be given the captain's chair? Forgive my impertinence. However, being your superior officer, it gives me the right to know the sort of man under my employ."

"Politics, sir," Darcy answered simply.

"You're going to have to give me more than that, Captain."

"Of course, Colonel. The truth is that I might have been too honest with my superiors. I have always preferred not to have officers served under me who are pressed into the army."

Colonel Forster leaned forward, surprised.

"You are against the idea of British subjects being forced into the army?" Forster repeated Darcy's concerns in simpler terms.

"I see the necessity of men performing their duty of serving our great empire, however, I prefer having soldiers who volunteered. They usually possess a greater capacity to perform their services more efficiently. And are less likely to desert and defect. When I preside over men who were forced to join the army, their heart is not in it as much."

Colonel Forster did not argue with this but understood Darcy's logic.

"While I don't agree with your sentiment, I can still comprehend your beliefs. Fair enough, but you will have many officers under your service who are pressed into being privates. Many good lieutenants have been produced that way. Besides, whether by choice or by force, young men need structure in their lives. Most crime happens in Britain from too many hands being idle."

"Crime happens anywhere because humans will be humans. And besides, we are not nearly as horrendous as our colonists."

"You're still young; you have not seen what I have seen. Either way, arrangements have been made for you. You'll be staying at Lieutenant Brampton's Headquarters. He will hand over command to you since my regiment must move outside of Boston to begin to inspect the New England countryside."

"Your orders are to start patrolling all roads between here and Connecticut, correct?"

"And to New Hampshire."

"What of Pennsylvania?" Darcy asked suddenly. "There is Philadelphia, which is one of the largest cities in the Empire."

"Philadelphia's main delegates are Quakers; they believe in non-violence, which is good in our favor—for once! They will be too confused over their principles being broken. Pennsylvania is no threat at all. This is a New England crisis, and Pennsylvania and New York will not be drawn into this."

Despite Darcy respecting Colonel Forster, he was dubious. Even though he hadn't been to Philadelphia in years, as well as him having no evidence for justifying his superstition, Darcy did not believe that Philadelphia and Pennsylvania were no threat to British retaliation to the uprisings. However, he didn't speak again because he worried of trying the Colonel's patience.

"I'll report my orders to Brampton," Darcy said, preparing to leave. "Before I go, I must ask. What sort of man is Brampton?"

Colonel Forster raised an eyebrow.

"He began as a good man who was impartial. But the constant conflicts with the Bostonians have worn him down. I believe him to be a good man underneath it all, but the fighting has broken him. And his sergeant as well, for that matter."

"His sergeant?"

"He is the main one that you will converse with. Like I said, the fighting has affected Brampton. Again, Brampton is honorable, but once he gets off his horse, he tends to shy away from anything to do with politics, strategy, and meetings. He sometimes prefers to convey his messages through his sergeant, which Brampton treats like that of batman."

"What's the sergeant's name?"

"Bingley. Charles Bingley."

CHAPTER 5
Soar & Salutations

"Eliza!" Charlotte Lucas cried from a window on Lucas Lodge's second floor.

When I dismounted the horse, I waved to her happily. The sun's gaze fell on her beautiful face, and I felt elated at her sight. Between her beauty and her present state of life aiming toward perfect matrimony, I sensed that her spirit rendered her loveliness even greater.

Collins placed my bags on the ground, and I felt a resignation radiate from him. Looking up at him, I saw the look in his eyes—it was a refusal.

"You aren't coming in, are you?" I deduced.

Collins looked down at me, a resentment that was mingled with sadness in his eyes.

"Believe me, Elizabeth. They will not receive me. I'm going to make it easier for the both of us." He egged his horse onward, preparing to turn him around. "Besides, I do not like going into a house where everyone frowns at my face. I leave that to stronger men. Do not worry about finding me; I have always been good at finding you."

Digging his heels into the horse's sides, he rode away, swiftly down the street.

His retreat could not have been done too soon or too late. Just as he disappeared down the road, Charlotte Lucas emerged out of the house.

Dropping my belongings, I rushed up to her and we embraced. Of being among friends again, I felt my spirit warm as Charlotte wrapped her arms around me.

"You came back!" she cried. "You came to see us."

"Of course, I did," I replied, chuckling. "You did not think that I would miss the special day for you?"

"Thank you. Weddings are often considered small affairs for us, but I still wanted you there."

"Small in *their* eyes, but who cares what anyone else thinks?" I responded archly, willing to scoff at the world. After all, I had done it so many times before, so what was one more scoff? "You know that's never held me down."

"No," Charlotte responded, smiling, "I daresay that you never have."

Suddenly, her eyes lost their luster, and her face and tone became serious.

"But Lizzy, I must ask. Are you still much as you have ever been? In your beliefs."

Inwardly, I sighed. What I was about to tell her would be something that she would not like to hear.

"Yes. In all essentials, I am as I have always been."

Charlotte's eyes filled with worry. Despite my inclinations and passions, I was not about to ruin her life. I didn't come to Boston for that.

"Charlotte," I assured her, "no matter what I feel about the Quakers who rejected me, I will not be a sore on your family."

"Promise?" she asked pleadingly.

I smiled—in the manner and habit that I always did when I felt defiantly amusing.

"Cross my heart and pledge my mind," I vowed.

"Good. I can believe that."

We finished our conversation at the correct time, because with the fall of Charlotte's last sentence, her brother Henry emerged from the house. Sir William Lucas and Lady Lucas had also come out to meet me, followed by two of their other small children.

Now was not the time for talks of revolution.

～

"Dear Miss Elizabeth!" Sir William boomed, emerging, and taking my hands eagerly. "It is a delight to see you."

"And it is so with you, Sir William," I replied, just as relieved to see him as he had been happy to see me. I felt his warmth radiate from within his soul and was happy for it. I needed a paternal air about me.

"How is Jane and spirited little Kitty?" Sir William asked. "Surely they must be married already, with their charms."

"Oh, you must not be disappointed," I uttered, "they are as single as I."

"Oh, well, no matter, no matter. They are just taking their time, as you are, I daresay."

"My dear, you are too much putting Miss Bennet on the spot," Lady Lucas countered. "One does not have to spend the day talking about beaus. Especially at this time."

For the first time, I was happy with Lady Lucas's reserved manner. Jane and Kitty remained in Philadelphia, and both suffered under the realities that life did not work out for them in the manner that we had hoped. And it was something that I had no choice but to inform everyone of.

Once the family met me, they brought me inside. As they did so, Henry Lucas looked at the street.

"Wasn't it Mr. Collins who rode you here?" he asked.

"Yes," I answered with trepidation, "he did."

Looking around at the rest of the family, I saw their shoulders slack under the reality that the bad experience had driven right past him.

"That was good of him," Sir William responded. "We can't afford to have the likes of men like him here."

"Because you both think so differently," I pointed out as Henry Lucas brought my luggage inside.

"No," Lady Lucas responded, "because of the arrivals."

When hearing her say that, I felt the apprehension of not knowing something that I ought to have known.

"The what?" I asked.

"The arrival of hundreds more British officers."

I bit my lip. Seeing me properly vexed, Lady Lucas grinned forcefully.

"Oh, here I am talking about things that one ought not to talk about when first visiting us."

"Elizabeth does not mind, my dear," Sir William countered. "If I do not mistake your character, Eliza, but you prefer to be kept abreast of news that has reached Boston."

"I would like to immediately," I supported as I entered their parlor. "I have the sense that I walked into a town that is about to be set on fire."

"Lizzy, you hyperbolize," Lady Lucas countered.

"Does she, Mother?" Charlotte asked as I sat down and I distinctly saw tea being presented to me, rather than coffee or chocolate. "Because troubles are ahead."

"And these acts are just the beginning," one of the smaller Lucas children uttered, who I recalled was little Sally. Knowing that she wanted to contribute to the conversation, I patted her head as she winked at me.

"What do the British intend to do in retaliation for the Boston Tea Party?" I questioned again.

Knowing that this would upset me, Charlotte's voice trembled somewhat as she explained.

"There is no solid evidence, but we have heard things. They are considering closing Boston to merchant shipping."

When hearing this, my eyes widened with shock.

"They might close down the Boston Harbor?" I blurted out without thinking.

"Well, yes. Mind you, it will be only done to punish the colonists for the constant rioting."

"And the harassment of Loyalists," Sir William added heatedly. "Do you know how many shops have been attacked because they support the crown? These so-called patriots are worse than the tyrant that they claim to be oppressing them. The hypocrisy is astounding."

While I acknowledged the evils of mob-rule, I still was not, and never would be, blind to how things had unfolded in the last few years. Both the Sons of Liberty and the British regulars did unspeakable things.

"Is that the extent of their retaliation?" I asked, though my question was hollow, at best. I was well aware that the repercussions to the Boston Tea Party did not end there, and naturally would not.

"Well, eventually the officers will need places to stay. We have heard talk that they might start having officers live in homes, without paying anything."

I squinted, realizing what they meant.

"A Quartering Act?" I summed up.

Heavily, Charlotte nodded her head. Looking around at the

rest of the Lucas family, I could not believe that they considered this honorable.

"That means that British troops can move into any house they want, eat all the colonists' food, take whatever they wish from the homes—and maybe even throw the Bostonians out of their own residences, if they want to use it for their headquarters," I defined.

"Yes," Lady Lucas replied. "But considering all the money that was lost from the tea being dumped into the harbor, the retaliation does make sense."

I took a look around the house.

"This is a lovely house," I noted. "One of the loveliest in the neighborhood."

"Thank you," Sir William replied, pride rising with him. His self-satisfaction rendered him good-natured, but not always the best at being deductive.

"Sir William, you do not understand my meaning," I furthered. "Your home is lovely, and it appears to all that you are a man of means. What happens when the British require things from you, even taking all the food from your cellars?"

"It is our duty to serve our officers," Sir William declared.

"But at the expense of running you into debtor's prison," I countered. "The Lucas family is legend in Boston. I don't want anything happening to you all. At the moment, any damages done cannot affect you now, but it can do so as time wears on. Besides, as you all say, the times are tense. If you are seen sympathizing with the soldiers, then how is it going to be when the rioters come after you?"

"More British officers are coming to our aid," Mr. Henry Lucas added. "They wouldn't dare get violent again."

I sighed.

"The one thing that I learned from life is that desperate men do not always think before they act."

I turned back to them all and saw the anxiousness on their faces.

"Pray, forgive me," I coaxed. "I haven't seen you in years, and I return, acting in this manner. I suppose that this is what you must assume I sound like when I am happy."

They all laughed, and I eased my way back into the group.

"My friend is getting married," I said.

"Yes, I am!" Charlotte declared, "everyday, in a few weeks."

"Then we ought to be happy for you. I must meet this man who claims to be good enough for my friend. What is the man's name? When you wrote to me in my letter, there was a water stain on where his name was, so I am still quite ignorant."

"Oh, you met him before," Charlotte added, alive with excitement. "It's Mr. MacDougall."

Never had I been good at names before, so it took a moment for me to recall.

"Alexander MacDougall," Charlotte said.

When hearing his first name, the man's face returned to me.

"Alexander MacDougall!" I responded, elated. "The Scotsman."

"Yes, that's him."

"And you were right, Charlotte," Little Sally said, reading my expression. "She knew that would make you happy."

"You're marrying one of my fellow countrymen," I remarked, elated.

"I did not intend it, but it all came to a natural conclusion that makes a great deal of sense," Charlotte responded.

"Oh," I replied with patriotic ease. "I remember Lex. Long-legged Lex."

"You're not going to call him that when you see him again, are you? He's trying to get past that name."

"Too late, he will always be Long-legged Lex to me.

Always was good at running away from us ladies whenever we made him nervous. Besides, he's my fellow Scot, so he should know what he's getting in for. I'm surprised that he ever had the courage to court a woman, let alone propose to one."

"He's found his courage," Charlotte responded, proud. "Oh, I cannot wait for you to see him, Lizzy. You would be amazed to see the transformation he's undergone."

"Well, the Earth was created in six days, so I am likely to believe in anything, at this point."

Next, I looked at Henry Lucas.

"And what of you, Henry?" I asked. "Are you free from the slavery that is falling in love?"

"Elizabeth!" Lady Lucas gasped. "Honestly! The things that you say! Falling in love is not a slavery."

"I cannot help but agree with Eliza," Henry Lucas responded. "She and I have both been thrown in and out of love enough that we cannot help but wonder if it's not for us."

Everyone gasped at this.

"Oh, that cannot be true!" Little Sally declared.

"It can," I replied, "you see, when it comes to love, I have been taken in so much, that now I am aware that I do not have the best of taste when it comes to choosing men to care for. Besides, Henry and I have reached an age where we have been so much living by our own habits and routine, that it feels strange to share that routine with anyone else."

"Precisely." Henry Lucas laughed. "Eliza, I think you and I are stuck in the proverbial rut!"

"And I welcome it," I agreed. "After my mistakes, never do I believe that I will ever let a love in my life."

~

After talking about Charlotte's fiancé, I was about to tell the Lucases the truth of how my family was, back in Philadelphia, when I realized that someone was missing.

"Maria?" I noted. "I cannot believe that I just realized, but Maria is not here. Is she visiting the Cramptons or the Forbes?"

The atmosphere in the room dropped significantly. As a point of fact, I could denote that I had quite ruined the comfort that we all had found again. Yet, it was not my fault, and would prove to be the first of my struggles when I returned to Boston.

"Maria is ill," Sir William said, his tone heavy. That was the first sign that I knew I had to feel the great dictator that was 'Death', creeping in. Sir William loved Maria. In fact, there were times that I always sensed that she was his favorite child.

"Ill?" I echoed, my voice equally as stony. "How ill?"

Sir William's eyes became even more downcast.

"She has a putrid sore throat."

I felt my stomach turn to lead.

"Putrid sore throat?" I repeated. "Are you certain?"

"The doctors have confirmed it."

"They have determined that it's a serious inflammation of the throat, the tonsils, and the folds of the palate," I described.

"Yes, they have."

I rubbed my lips, then folded my arms over my chest.

"Did they see any gangrene patches in the throat?" I asked.

The family looked at each other, and ignorance was in their eyes.

"The doctor didn't check for that?" I asked.

"No, he did not mention it."

Well, that does it.

Standing up, I went to the stairs.

"Get some broth prepared, and pull out the horehound and honey," I said, taking the steps two at a time. "I must see her immediately."

"Splendid," Sir William said, jumping up as Lady Lucas began to do as I bade. "Eliza, you should have arrived three days ago."

"Forgive me," I replied, reaching the upper landing, and talking to him over my shoulder. "Sadly, I was too poor for that."

I went to tend to Maria Lucas.

I prayed that I was not too late.

CHAPTER 6
An Officer & a Gentleman

When Captain Darcy arrived at Lieutenant Brampton's headquarters near the Boston Harbor, Darcy looked around the street, marking what homes and businesses were near the headquarters, and what was the likeliest places for which a mob would charge the building, if such a situation would occur.

When he entered and was presented, he was prepared for Brampton's absence.

However, what he was not prepared for was to enter seeing a sergeant at a desk, with his head resting on the wooden surface, a bottle of brandy next to him and the room a little unkempt.

The sight was abominable, and naturally made Darcy's blood boil. He informed his escort to leave him, wishing to undertake this trial alone. He was going to scream at this sergeant, and thought it correct to let the man be berated in a private sort of way. Taking a nearby sheep-haversack that was on a chair, Darcy hurled it at the man's head.

This had the desired effect.

The man shook, having been woken up so physically. He rolled his head as he raised it up and rubbed his eyes.

"Ah, you're awake," Darcy uttered. "Forgive me for interrupting the lack of professionalism that I am being met with."

Not only had the man been sleeping, suffering from being somewhat drunk, but his military jacket was off, laying clumsily on a footstool, his necktie was loosened, and his waistcoat was partly unbuttoned.

The man stood, trying to steady himself against the table.

"My apologies, sir."

"I assume that you do that a great deal," Darcy replied, his eyes filled with wrath.

The man laughed nervously, but there was something more to it. In the man's laugh, there was a hint of sadness. When studying the sergeant's appearance, he must've been in his late twenties—or looked younger than he was. His frame was neither sturdy, nor slight. His build denoted an active man, but not a bulky one.

As the sergeant scrambled around to make himself more presentable, arranging his regimentals, Darcy was at his wit's end.

"Captain Fitzwilliam Darcy, reporting to Brampton's regiment, and assume command. State your name and rank, sir. And stand at attention!"

The man stood erect, assuming some professionalism.

"Sergeant Charles Bingley, of the Light Calvary," Mr. Bingley responded. "At your service, Captain."

'So, this is the sergeant who is to be my eyes and ears,' Darcy thought.

Already, the situation looked bleak.

Removing his tricorn hat, and placing it on a cabinet against the wall, Darcy did not look at Bingley as he spoke.

"Sergeant Bingley, I presume you are aware how you appear to me now."

"Yes, sir," Bingley responded, "I have an inkling."

"An inkling?" Darcy looked Bingley up and down. "Yes, I presume that you use that word a great deal."

Bingley rolled his lip in his mouth and still stared ahead.

"I come to assume command, and this is what I find," Darcy announced, pacing around Bingley. "A lieutenant who is missing and a sergeant who is drunk. This is a level of lewdness and unprofessional behavior that has no place in his Majesty's service. With the arrival of new officers to surveil the Boston harbor, I am quite certain that I could find a better sergeant and informant than what stands before me now."

"I understand, sir," Bingley responded, shame etched across his eyes. "Am I to be relieved entirely of my position? I acknowledge how I must appear as always being now."

"How you must appear?" Darcy hissed. "This behavior is unpardonable." Not only was the man unkempt, but the desk was also filthy, covered with papers. "Before you are removed from my sight, you will clean this space, and—" Darcy picked up one of the papers and Bingley's eyes widened in alarm.

"No!" Bingley cried, reaching out to the paper.

Seeing the man's devastation, Darcy looked down at the paper that was in his hand. The sergeant's reaction piqued his curiosity and Darcy had no choice but to raise the paper and began to read:

… Bingley, I apologize to be the bringer of such news, cousin, but Helena fell ill and was taken from this earth. Her illness was longstanding, and therefore we can now say that she is at peace.

I am aware of the crushing blow that you have been dealt, and the pain of losing such a great passion to your life.

Helena is now with God, and soon, who shall tend to her, until you both can be reunited in the vastness of heaven...

Darcy lowered the letter, immediately feeling the shame of reading so private a missive.

However, in the next minute, his regrets faded as he looked at the disheveled and drunken man, the brandy bottle on the desk, and the letter in his hand.

"Helena?" Darcy uttered. "Who is she to you?"

Bingley breathed in heavily.

"My wife. She was my wife."

～

When hearing that, everything became apparent. Darcy's personality shifted, immediately transferring from resentment to sympathy. The man had lost his wife.

"What happened?" Darcy asked slowly. "Was she with child?"

For if that were to be so, then his sergeant not only lost his wife, but perhaps also lost a newborn.

"No," Bingley answered simply, his eyes somewhat red. "She was taken by fever and a whooping cough. She died a couple months ago, but it was not until last week that I received the news. I should have thrown the letter away..."

"But you kept it," Darcy finished his sentence, "hoping it's a lie."

"Yes." Bingley looked at him with curiosity. "How did you discover such?"

"I made an assumption."

"I know I ought to," Bingley said heavily, "but I... I just cannot bring myself to dispose of the letter."

Once again, Darcy analyzed his new sergeant, only this time, he was looking at him with new eyes. He was looking at a man who lost the most important woman in his life. Assuming he could drown his worries in drink, but it only augmented the problem.

Darcy closed the brandy bottle, went over to the fireplace, and looked into the flames.

"Sergeant, retire to your room for an hour and then return to me in proper attire and with all your laces buttoned."

"Aye, Captain," Bingley responded, leaving the room swiftly.

When alone, Darcy cleaned up the room himself, determined to do the man a kindness. After he was finished, he sat down, leaned back, and stared out of the window.

If he weren't aware of all that he was about to face, he would say that he was met with a bittersweet image. Boston was a lovely city, until he knew why he was there.

"Fitzwilliam," he said to himself, "you come to a post where the dangers are everywhere, to a lieutenant who is away, a colonel who will be gone, and to a sergeant who is devastated. Welcome back to Massachusetts."

An hour later, a few batmen had brought in all of Darcy's luggage, assembled them in his room, and brought in all his information and maps to study the Boston city again. Since he had not been there in four years, the city had expanded, and he had to know his territory better than he knew the back of his hand.

As he was doing so, there was a knock on his door, and he knew what to expect.

"Come in, Bingley."

The door opened and Sergeant Bingley entered. Dressed pristinely, his regimentals unwrinkled, his cap straight, his waistcoat and half-gaiters all clean, his hair combed and tied back in a black ribbon, he presented himself.

"Have you had time to recover from hard drink?" Darcy asked, still pouring over the map.

"Yes, sir," Bingley responded. "As much as I regret to mention how I appeared an hour ago, but the sleep relieved me of the effects."

Darcy arched his eyebrow.

"I can well believe that. Remain at attention."

"Aye, sir."

At last, Darcy sat back down and finally looked at Bingley. From all appearances, Charles Bingley seemed to be a respectable-looking man. Although, he had to make certain that this was not his usual habit, and that such acts would never be repeated.

"In the hour since you and I have met, I've spoken with other officers and aid-de-camps who have de-briefed me on the situation. They have informed me that you are not usually like this."

"I truly do believe in doing my duty, captain. I just…"

"Yes. I am—" Darcy trailed off. He didn't know how he was going to say what he did, because he was always a bit awkward when it came to these situations. "I am aware that nothing that I say will ease the pain of what you are enduring. I cannot begin to understand how your heart aches. But I am sorry for your loss."

"Thank you. You are the first one."

"The first one?"

"The first to acknowledge that you don't know what I am feeling. We men are supposed to carry on, but I have never possessed that talent."

"I suppose that it shows how real that it was."

"Thank you. It's just…"

"What?"

"I wasn't there," Bingley said heavily. "I was not there when she died. I was here, far away from her. I could not be there to say that I loved her. That I regret perhaps not doing enough."

"In those circumstances, there is nothing that you can do."

"I know, but you still cannot help but feel such guilt. It's natural, I suppose. But there it is. And when we parted, it was pleasant, but it was not overtly affectionate. After all, I knew that I would return and that we would see each other again. I… you never know when your last moment with someone will be your last moment with them."

"I suppose I can understand that as well. And that revelation hit you hard, at this present moment."

"It did. I just felt as if my heart went somewhere else."

"Again, I am sorry. But I need you to always be at your best, sergeant. This can never happen again."

"Thank you, sir. It never will."

The shift was incredible.

When first meeting Bingley, Darcy had wished the man to be on the other side of the world.

However, now that he knew the man's history, the reverse had occurred. Darcy felt an immediate affection for him. Even though they were quite different, Bingley felt like a kindred spirit.

It also sparked an even greater prejudice toward the New England colonists. If it weren't for all these uprisings, Bingley would never have been brought to America, to bring order to the chaos and help suppress the violence of the rebellions. He would have been back home, in England, and at least could have been with his wife when she left for the next world that was beyond.

This presented an even further resentment to what was happening.

Shutting away these theories, he returned to his present situation.

"Now," Darcy said, "I have read Brampton's notes. He is doing well to uphold curfew, but I wish to go further than that. I need officers to patrol all the main streets, but I also would like disguised officers, in regular dress, go into taverns and discover what is being planned. Groups like the Sons of Liberty sometimes have been known to meet in such places."

"A good plan. Permission to speak freely."

"Freely, yes. Offensively, no."

"Be prepared for not as much news on that venture. Now that our response to the Tea Party is so powerful, I feel that they will go even further into the shadows."

"Noted. We need informants. I also want a list of all the loyalists in the area, as well as those who are known to be neutral in this fight. Those can also be vital at reporting the mood of the town and the impact that they will have on the other colonies."

"This is a New England uprising."

"Are you aware that I was present when their so-called 'Boston Massacre' occurred?"

"I was briefed on that, yes, captain."

"After the tragedy, a man named Paul Revere drew a painting that awoke the empathy throughout the colonies. This conflict is starting in New England, but revolution has a way of being a concept that is contagious. I know that it is believed that this problem will remain in Massachusetts, but mark my words, things will spread. I don't predict that this problem will be dismissed quickly."

"You think that we shall be here longer?"

"I know it."

Two hours later, Bingley returned with a list of the men who were rumored to be the Sons of Liberty.

As Darcy began to look over the list, Bingley remained talking.

"While the self-proclaimed Sons of Liberty are behind so many of our conflicts," Bingley began, "our sources believe that many people despise their activities. They have more enemies in Boston than we do."

"No!" Darcy blurted out, while reading the list of the treasonous characters who were in the Sons' group.

"Captain?" Bingley asked.

Bingley's voice might have felt like it was from miles away.

One of the names on the list was all too familiar to him:

Richard Fitzwilliam

His cousin's name was among those on the list of the Sons of Liberty.

CHAPTER 7

A Search for Herbs & Healing

As I followed Charlotte and Lady Lucas up the stairs, with Little Sally following after us, I wondered how far Maria's illness was. After all, I had seen Putrid Sore Throat before, and the effects could be fatal. It could also lead to a whooping cough, and that could easily be the end of it.

We approached Maria's bedroom, Charlotte knocked, warned her of my entry, and we opened the door. As I entered, the curtains were closed, for the sake of the sun, not disturbing Maria's rest.

Maria's head turned and rose from her pillow, but was too weak to do anything else but remove one arm from under the covers.

In her face were all the signs of a woman who was very ill.

"Lizzy," Maria said.

I rushed to her bed, sat down next to her, and I began to press her neck.

"Aye, Maria, I arrived in Boston safe and sound. Does this pressure make you feel any pain?"

"Yes," she replied, referring to my caressing her neck, "not too much, but it still does hurt."

Removing a handkerchief from my under-pocket that was hidden under the sides of my petticoat, I covered my mouth with it.

"You all ought to do the same," I advised Charlotte and Lady Lucas.

Charlotte did as I instructed, but Lady Lucas naturally was dubious. After all, she was the older one, and was less prone to me giving orders. Or anyone younger than her, for that matter.

"I don't see what covering our mouths would do."

"I still hold fast to my belief that an illness can be contagious simply by breath. When being too close to someone who is ill, you can catch it. There's a reason that those who've had the Yellow Fever were shut away from others."

"Well, my daughter is ill, and I do not have time to care for such notions."

I rolled my eyes.

Still with my mouth and nose covered, I looked at Maria, wiped the sweat down her face and took in her loss of color.

"Well, I have one set of good news, Maria," I said. "You are romantically pale, like all the heroines you love to read about."

Maria chuckled but coughed immediately afterwards. This was not a good sign.

"Maria," I said as I went to the bedstand and got a candle, "I need you to open your mouth, so that I can inspect your throat."

I lit the candle as she opened her mouth, placed one of my fingers near the wick so that I saw deep within. Inwardly, I sighed, as it was worse than what I thought.

"Yes," I confirmed. "Yes."

"Your yeses can be very hard," Charlotte uttered, sitting next to me. "What does that mean?"

"Is the horehound and honey almost finished being heated up?" I asked.

"Yes."

"That does well. It is not just enough for it to be placed in tea. She needs to drink it raw and heated. It will coat her throat until I've acquired what is needed."

"What is it, Lizzy?" Maria asked, her voice hoarse.

I gave her a look, wondering if I should lie to her. But I was not very good at being deceptive, having never acquired that talent.

"Lizzy?" Maria repeated. "What's the point of lying to me? I already feel horrible. Am I to die? Is that what you are about to tell me?"

"While I do not determine Life and Death," I added, "I suppose you've quite dissembled me. It's a shame. I was really hoping to lie." Keeping my voice calm so not to rouse her, I began to unfold it. "Maria, you have all the symptoms of the Putrid. Your throat and tonsils are inflamed. The redness is extreme. The mucous is building, and there are patches in the throat." I looked at Lady Lucas and Charlotte. "If the blood vessels in this area of her throat begin to hemorrhage, the illness can be fatal."

A servant came into the room with the warm horehound and honey. As Maria drank it, I gave my next direction.

"Now boil some water, fill it with salt, and I'll consult with Dr. Warren," I said, "I'm surprised that he isn't here, with how terrible her condition is."

"Eliza," Lady Lucas gasped. "You cannot go to Dr. Warren."

I looked at her, confused.

"What are you talking about?" I asked, flabbergasted. Looking at all the women, a thought came to me. "You never went to Dr. Warren, have you?"

"We could not," Charlotte acknowledged. "As much as I would prefer to."

"Prefer to? Then why didn't you?" I looked between them both. "Is there something that I am missing?"

"He's a part of the rebellion," Maria Lucas said hoarsely, "we cannot speak to him."

"Dr. Warren? He's a patriot?"

"Don't use that word," Lady Lucas said. "They are traitors is what they are. We have it upon good authority, Elizabeth, that he's involved with the Sons of Liberty. He's a part of all the violence."

The blood within me ran cold as I held another secret within me. I was a patriot.

Truly, I was aware of their loyalist sympathies, and I bore no ill will towards them. But I was wholly unaware that their loyalist preferences led to such an extreme prejudice. They would not even let the best doctor in Boston attend Maria.

And I had come to stay for a time. I was stricken with a sudden premonition that my time in New England was not going to end well. In fact, I felt as if a crushing end was descending upon me where I would be set down in disgrace.

Either way, I had a sick patient on my hands and there was a doctor who could help.

"Dr. Warren could save Maria," I insisted. "We must bring him here."

"If we do that," Lady Lucas said, "then we will be considered as consorting with traitors. We cannot do that, especially with all that is occurring. There is no room for inconsistencies."

I was angry, but also able to see the logic of this. More British troops were arriving by the day. They were constantly on the streets, and there were eyes everywhere.

"I can go to Dr. Warren," I said. "I am an outsider."

"But you are staying with us," Charlotte informed me. "You can be traced back to Lucas Lodge."

"Even if I could, I could be pardoned. I'm a Pennsylvanian. I would not know any better."

Patience was never one of my virtues. I didn't like it when things took very long. As such, I was not in the mood to sit here and be inactive.

"It all matters to what you prefer. Your reputation, or Maria's life?"

This had the desired effect. We were living in complicated times, but this matter was simple.

"I'll walk myself," I replied, putting the blankets further around Maria's neck. "I'll return soon."

Leaving Lucas Lodge before I had to cross paths with Sir William and Henry Lucas, I knew that Dr. Warren's home was not far away.

Since it had eventually become a warm day, I was able to walk without my cloak on, so I went out into the warm air.

It was strange; I had come to Boston to see friends, but there is never anything comparable to being out in the open air. And, despite that I would always prefer being home in Philadelphia, Boston still had its own quaintness to it. It was not as large as where I was from, but the difference was not a negative.

And the city had done well at rebuilding since its fire years ago.

Occasionally, I crossed paths with a few British troops. I had assumed that if I was amiable, smiled and nodded to them, then I would be left alone.

However, no military is without its uncouth characters. Some of the soldiers smiled and nodded to me. But other times, I was stopped, interrogated, and asked where I was headed. I was honest, and that did not do me very many favors. It was natural to be suspicious of anyone and everyone, so they asked to search my market wallet—thank goodness I had learned to always keep my money in my pockets under my petticoat. When they only found a handkerchief, some smelling salts, and an apple in there, they let me press on.

With the first British guards who stopped me, it was a 'Very well, good day to you, Miss. Sorry to have kept you.'

With the second set, it was 'A woman should not be out on the streets by herself. You're embarrassing yourself by walking alone like this. Don't be getting into any trouble. Treason on a girl is as ugly as treason on a man.'

Eventually, I did arrive at Dr. Warren's home and knocked on the door.

It opened and I smiled to see the familiar face that I was a kindred spirit with.

"Miss Elizabeth!" Dr. Warren proclaimed.

"Good day, Dr. Warren," I said.

"Oh, what a delight this is! Pray, do come in."

"With all the speed of Hermes," I replied, stepping in and him shutting the door behind me.

Dr. Warren had a very kind face and non-threatening appearance. Wearing a powdered wig that was simple and not ostentatious, he showed the signs of a man clinging to respectable gentility, but not flamboyance. He was of a medium height and build and looked every bit of a doctor as a man in his profession could appear as.

"My word, Miss Elizabeth, I didn't know you had come to Boston. Are your sisters with you?"

"They remain in Philadelphia, seeing to the remains of what our lives are."

Dr. Warren squinted when hearing this.

"The remains?" he repeated.

I sighed.

"It's strange. I come at the Lucases request, and you're the first one that I felt comfortable telling this to."

"What?" Dr. Warren said, going to his decanter and pouring me some brandy. He knew that I always preferred a little brandy with heavy conversation.

"Father is dead."

When hearing that, Dr. Warren almost dropped the glass he was about to hand me.

"What!" He gasped.

"Yes." My breath inside of me felt heavy as the coldness of being an orphan had rushed back into my heart. "Our father died."

Dr. Warren's face reminded me of Jane and Kitty's face when we remained at father's deathbed. And for all that I knew, it also could have been how I looked as well.

"Mr. Bennet was not very old," he uttered, "and when he last wrote to me, he never mentioned any illness."

"Because there was none. He suffered from a sudden apoplectic fit."

"Perhaps it was what some of us are considering to be a stroke," Dr. Warren noted. "Our findings are not conclusive in any way yet, and there is no set term for it. But it sounds like such. It can happen very suddenly. Or it can happen in reaction to something."

"It was. Father never recovered from when our mother died. It broke him. He had us, and that helped carry him on for a longer time. But mother was everything to him."

"Yes. She was his heart, wasn't she?"

"Yes, she was. They loved each other very much, and when

she died, a part of him died with her. And now they are togeth-er." Taking a sip from my cup, I let the memories wash over me, but did my best to not give into the despair that was natural and inevitable.

When three sisters lose their mother, they lose a strong emotional ally, as our mother had been. Especially since our mother had undergone hell and back to get to America when she left Scotland.

And when three sisters lose a father, they lose all protection and stability in the household.

"I cannot begin to imagine what Kitty, Jane, and you are undergoing right now. For a woman to lose a father—"

"Yes," I finished, "and a father like ours." I sighed, giving into sadness. "He believed in us, you must understand. He wanted so much for us. And not just to get married."

"Mr. Bennet was one of the best men in our profession. What will happen to his practice?"

"That was another hard thing. Father was hoping, when he died, we would have already had enough training and gained enough people's trust for them to want to come to us. But that's not what happened. He died earlier than he would have wanted, and now we lose the house, the apothecary shop, and practice he set up. No one will come to us. In their eyes, we were just his assistants, and therefore, we could not help that at all."

"I cannot begin to understand what you are feeling now," Dr. Warren empathized. "Though I confess to not being entirely surprised. After a few years of you being born, your father wrote to my family about his predicament. To be a father who cares, and have daughters born into a world where, if something were to happen to him, he worried about what would happen to you all. To have children like his, and never given the chance to be *given* equal chances. He always worried about that and was embarrassed over it."

Hearing this surprised me. Leaning forward, I put my cup down and desired to know more immediately.

"He was?" I asked.

"Yes, he was. He never told you?"

I shook my head.

"I can understand why," Warren added, "it's something that men only talk about in close confidence with other men. And maybe to their wives. Well, if they like their wives…"

I laughed sadly.

"Elizabeth, if it's not too bold to call you such… I am sorry, but perhaps I can help you. Massachusetts and Pennsylvania may be two different worlds, but I still have friends there. I can write to the Darraghs, the Drinkers, and Benjamin Rush."

"You know Benjamin Rush?" I asked, astounded.

"I do. We have written back and forth many times. If I can get him to speak on your behalf, then he might be willing to encourage people that Mr. Bennet's daughters are following in his footsteps. Though, he is a businessman and is very likely to not want the competition."

"I'm a woman; what threat do I pose?"

Mr. Warren raised an eyebrow.

"A great deal of competition. Why do you think man has always placed you where he has?"

I was not alarmed by this speech, but merely happy that he was willing to be brave and speak about it.

"Is that what you believe?"

"I cannot say for certain, but I cannot help but wonder. Either way, at the very least, he can have you Bennet girls as his assistants."

"Anything is better than nothing," I said, happier to have come. "Father raised us to be doctors and surgeons. We don't know how to do much else."

"I'll write to him today."

I smiled… until I recalled why I had come.

~

After mentioning Maria Lucas's condition, Dr. Warren was upset, to say the least.

"Your diagnosis is clearly correct, from what you mentioned. Putrid Sore Throat. Sir William and Lady Lucas are being foolish. The child ought to be properly seen to. My political views are not more important than her health."

"Thus is the pain of choosing sides," I replied, finishing my brandy. "No one can see that differences of opinion do not mean difference of morals."

"Well, I am glad to see that you have kept your wits about you and do not care who I associate with."

"My preferences for you is natural… because we share the same values."

Dr. Warren's expression changed when he discovered that my feelings for our fight for equality had still gone unchallenged.

"You do?"

"Yes. I will never condone the violence, on both sides. I neither agree with it being the order of the day, nor will I accept that as an adequate means to achieve it. They are not what I believe in."

"Nor do I," he insisted. "I can assure you. Some of us do believe that our liberties can be obtained in a much better manner. I just… I had assumed that you would have changed your feelings after the Boston Massacre."

"I still stand by the British soldiers being innocent for defending themselves. But there were colonists, Crispus Attucks and George Hughes who had real reasons, real complaints to speak of." I rubbed my head. "Life is so complicated, isn't it?"

"Yes. It is."

"Well, one thing is simple. Maria is ill and the Lucases can't come to you of their own accord. Due to their own sympathies. First, it's best that I am their intermediary, for now. And secondly, I know that it might be best for me to have to leave that house soon."

"Why?"

"It's only a matter of time before they find out that I've aligned myself in a different direction. They would not want to put me out, but they would feel obliged to. I refuse to have allegiance to a king that cannot even exert himself to visit his colonists. It's obvious; in his eyes, the Prime Minister's eyes, and Parliaments' eyes, and many others, we are not considered equal. And I fear that we never will be. They view us all as an inferior species, and I will not abide it. We have just cause to be angry. But the fact is that I need money to take me home again and book passage on any ship that will take me back to Philadelphia. Do you know any taverns that would take me on as a scullery maid, or anyone who needs a chambermaid for a duration? I need to provide for myself when I am here."

Dr. Warren leaned back and analyzed me.

"At this time of year, I have many clients, and there is always someone with fever, whooping coughs, and even a case of typhus here and there. I could do with an assistant."

Smiling was the best I could offer. Truly, this was better than I could have hoped for!

"You would do that for me?"

His eyes twinkled.

"As one patriot to another."

~

"But we must return to Maria Lucas," Dr. Warren continued, offering to assist me. "You also know to use apple cider vinegar."

"And for her to gurgle salt water, but I worry it's too late."

"It's never too late for salt water. It purifies. Just keep it warm. But there is also a matter to do with the pain she is undergoing. Crushing down bark and turning it into a pill state will enhance her chances."

"Bark?" I questioned, dubious. "Yes, it can dull pain, but that's only with Peruvian bark, or Jesuits Bark. But that's to deal with fevers."

"It's rare to know this, but I've been doing some experiments, and the willow tree near Pike's Stream has proven to sometimes help with pain relief. It helps the patient endure the illness."

"You're referring to the Tree of Human Souls," I replied, uneasy. Immediately my blood ran cold at considering that we got something that was so important to the Indians. Naturally, Dr. Warren heard the edge in my voice and noted my resentment.

"Still mistrustful of Indians?" he asked.

"What choice do I have?" I blurted out, bitter. "How can I trust them? Not after all that I have seen and befriended so many of their victims!"

Dr. Warren knew not to argue with me. He knew my past, and what I had endured. There were some scars that went too deep, too permanent. I could never befriend an Indian and never wanted to see one again. I thanked him for not pressing the matter.

"Well," he uttered, "I know that you know how to ground the bark into powder. Once put into that state, mix it with tea. Give it to Maria Lucas to drink, then have her gurgle salt water afterwards."

I grinned, happily.

"Splendid."

I stood up to leave, aiming to go to the Tree of Human Souls, and Dr. Warren sensed that I was about to depart, and his brow furrowed.

"You are aiming to go now?" he asked.

"Aye," I replied. "As you and I both know, time is of the essence."

"Yes, I concur," he agreed, "but I cannot close my shop early to assist you, for I have patients, and cannot permit you to go, unescorted."

"I made it to Massachusetts without suffering even a scratch," I replied, chuckling. "I can survive going to a tree." As soon as I had said it, my mind shifted, and then I realized something. "Indians don't still hunt near there, do they?"

"Not anymore. It's too close to colonists. But anything can happen, and—"

"And I don't want to be captured and enslaved," I replied, rubbing my lips frustrated. How easy it is to forget the realities that one is new towards. "In Philadelphia, one does not have to worry about that any longer. We drove them back."

"But was it fair to?" Dr. Warren asked me, and I sensed the empathy that he was feeling for them. With a quick succession, memories fell over my thoughts of meeting too many people who were killed or captured under Indian raids. But one thing was certain: I was not responsible for what came before me.

"I cannot answer for how things were before I was born," I replied, "but what is in my control is what is present. Tell that to the Indians. I am not in the mood to suffer for the previous generations' mistakes of how they treated the Indians. So, I will make no excuse for them."

Once more, Dr. Warren did not argue with me, knowing that

it was hopeless. And begging your pardon, but I knew precisely what to think, and precisely what I was about.

We were interrupted by a knock on the door.

I sighed. That was enough to break the tension.

"Come in," Dr. Warren called, and the door opened, where a gentleman entered, removing his hat, and pulling the hair off his face that had fallen from his ribbon.

When seeing him, my eyes brightened when glimpsing a familiar face.

"Ah," Dr. Warren announced, his eyes lighting up like mine, "how timely met."

"I agree," I replied, and the man turned to me. When seeing me, he smiled, and approached me.

"Miss Bennet! Well, as I live and breathe."

"Good day, Colonel Fitzwilliam."

An old acquaintance of mine—who I enjoyed the company of very much but was never around long enough to call him a longtime friend—had entered. As is the way with certain individuals, his presence had an immediate effect of lessening the weight of any moment of pressure, and even the sun felt as if it fell into the room, brighter.

When hearing me call him such, Colonel Fitzwilliam chuckled and stepped forward.

"Still calling me Colonel?" he asked.

"It's a habit," I replied.

"A habit I like, even years after my resignation." He turned to Dr. Warren. "You never told me that the Bennet sisters had come?"

"I didn't know until she graced my shop with her presence. But your arrival is perfect." Dr. Warren reached into his desk and took out a parcel. Despite that he handed it to the Colonel quickly, I believed that I was able to see the name on it correctly: Revere.

"Miss Bennet needs to go to Pike's Stream and collect some bark," Dr. Warren said. "Do you have anything scheduled for today?"

"I only planned to visit Mr. Cole, but I never specified a time. Miss Bennet, please allow me to accompany you."

"With pleasure," I replied. "I don't have my pistols with me. So, I need all the assistance I can get."

He raised an eyebrow, amused.

"Was I wrong to teach you how to shoot?" he asked me.

"Never regret that!"

He laughed, offering me his arm, which I took eagerly. Placing the parcel in his haversack bag, he led me to the door.

"Dr. Warren, I shall see you tomorrow," Colonel Fitzwilliam called over his shoulder.

"Till tomorrow, sir."

I also bid farewell to Dr. Warren as we closed the door behind us and stepped out onto the street.

When doing so, I would have thought that my companion would offer some sort of shield from any suspicion. However, soon into walking down the street, we passed British soldiers who were patrolling the road, and I felt Colonel Fitzwilliam's arm tense up as we passed them.

I looked at his face, saw a swift animosity flash across his eyes before it was masked by a façade of pleasantness. He nodded to the British officers and greeted them.

Naturally, with his very eloquent and aristocratic accent, the British officers were aware that they were meeting a fellow native Englishman, and so we were able to sojourn onward, happily.

But I knew.

Even if I had not already seen the parcel, I knew.

Although this was neither the time nor place to address it.

Instead, I was determined to shift his attention toward safer topics of discussion.

"How does the Colonel do?" I asked.

"I would say better than ever," Colonel Fitzwilliam replied. He gestured to the city around him. "But as you can see, the times, Miss Bennet, the times!"

"Yes, it is."

"However," Colonel Fitzwilliam replied, "no matter what the circumstances, you know the sort of man that I am."

"Where there is a will, there's a way," I stated, recalling his slogan.

"Always. The one benefit that the Boston Tea Party has enacted is a chance for something else."

"Your tavern is doing well?" I asked him.

"Better than well!" he replied. "I took a chance and invested in something else that is now rising to prominence. I've started serving coffee at my tavern."

"Coffee!" I replied, astounded. "You started selling that?"

"Yes, I have. It's ghastly stuff, and at first, the colonists are not accustomed to it. However, coffee is not taxed in the brutal way, by the British Parliament. Literally, once word reached all the colonies about the Tea Party, many are now resisting drinking tea, and have switched to coffee. My gamble paid off, and coffee is served at my tavern, and has been quite the success. Who would have thought that political conflict could shift the world of drinks?"

"I never would have," I replied. "Even in Philadelphia, coffee is now rising, much to my surprise. I wonder how long it will last. After all, fashions come out as quickly as they come in."

"I do so hope it lasts the year. However, at the speed that

fashions do come and go, it might be a trend, and then fade into non-existence. Coffee—a drink that will probably not last. Dear lord, I hope I am wrong. What do you think of coffee?"

"I admit that I still prefer to drink chocolate the most, due to the health benefits. But *Kitty* and Jane love it the most."

After specifically emphasizing Kitty's name, I gave Colonel Fitzwilliam a side glance. When hearing her name, his expression shifted, becoming less casual and more alert and alive. I was curious. So very curious.

"How are your sisters?" he asked, trying to keep his voice calm. However, I was neither in the mood nor the mentality to be indirect. After all, I was not the one in love, so I had the benefit of being allowed to be direct.

"Colonel, there is no need to dance around what is most dear for you to get to the heart of."

He chuckled bashfully.

"Still brave at being direct?" he asked.

"Why not?"

Colonel Fitzwilliam rubbed his cheek.

"It would be faster if we go to my home, get my horse and ride to Pike's Stream. That would be faster."

"Yes, it would," I replied, disheartened. "Thank you."

We turned a corner and headed toward his house, which was right next to his tavern.

"And I see that you have done your best to avoid the subject at hand," I said. "Very well. I suppose we ought to. However, one must know certain things. If you have no wish to ever visit Philadelphia again, then it is best that Kitty knows. She will cry for a time, but I know that she will recover."

When hearing this, Colonel Fitzwilliam looked at me sharply.

"She's still in love with me?"

"Well, yes, if you must know." I didn't fear betraying

Kitty's confidence, because, despite my reservations about letting her be too open at showing her emotions, she would have wanted Colonel Fitzwilliam to still know this. "It's not her fault, you must understand. You did everything to have made her fall in love with you. But she is also aware of how men of the world can be."

"Elizabeth, you are insulting me."

"It's not insulting to say things as they usually are. There is nothing wrong for that. Let us speak in truths then. People have been known to fall in love, then time and distance separates those two and the heart changes. It's better to break Kitty's heart now, rather than to let her continue to dote on you. If you care about her, then give her that chance."

"I'm still in love with her."

When hearing that, I felt relief wash all over my sensations and I felt the assurance of a good man loving one of my sisters. Especially since all three of us Bennet sisters were not great beauties, by any means.

"You are?" I asked, hopeful.

"Aye, I am," he replied. "I confess, there was a time where I did fall out of love with her when I returned home. You are right; I am a man of the world. My apologies for you confronting me on that reality about myself."

"You are forgiven."

"It's a habit of some of us men; even when we know that we are wrong, we will still argue that we are right."

"Well, I will own that we women can be the same."

"Thank you."

"Not me, of course. I am *always* right."

"Nonsensical girl," he objected, laughing.

"As you were, as you were, as you were," I teased.

"Well, to be truthful, I did fall in love with another woman for a time."

"What happened?" I asked, perversely curious.

"Eliza, you're going to hate me."

"Too late, I already might if you keep stalling."

"It was not that I lost my love for her, but she lost her love for me."

"Ah," I remarked. "She chose another man over you."

"Yes, she did. I never made her an offer, nor did I ever press any physical affection on her. I was patient and took my time. The other man was faster."

"How did that make you feel?"

"Angry for a month. Sad in the second month. And then… I was no longer upset. My heartache lasted no more than two months. And my affections for Kitty returned."

Colonel Fitzwilliam chuckled.

"It's amazing how we can assume that infatuation means love," he continued, "but it is not. It's just a bit of affection coming through your heart and leaving quickly. In fact, my anger of her not choosing me had nothing to do with my heart being bruised, but only my pride. No one likes to be rejected."

"And so, your emotions turned back to Kitty."

"You despise me."

"Finish the story and answer the question. And then I will decide if I hate you."

"Kitty and I… well, it's been a year since I saw her. I didn't know if she still loves me."

"She does. She's written that she does."

"I know. But it's been five months since she has written."

"Due to the problems with British occupation, most letters are going astray."

"I know. I keep telling myself that, but so it is. When it

comes to love, paranoia enters the soul, and you begin to doubt if they take you seriously."

Embittered, I had the instinct to lash out. However, nothing could be gained from me being harsh to him. Ergo, I knew it was best to be calm in how I spoke.

"If your instinct was to blame Kitty for this sense of absence, you were wrong, Colonel. In fact, we women have the habit of dwelling longer on missing the man than the reverse. I don't care what literature says. We are not fickle, as it is written, but simply move on when it is time to do so. The era of women wasting their lives because one romance came to a tragic end is prehistoric, if you ask me."

"I know," he replied, grudgingly. "I know. However, it was hard upon me. The distance between us hurts. And it *hurt* me. So, I tried to move on, as you say. I was wrong. But—Kitty truly loves me still? After all this time."

"She never forgot you. I think, no matter what happens to you, that you will forever be the great love of her life."

Colonel Fitzwilliam's eyes sparkled.

That made me happy.

We reached his house and tavern, The Green Dragon.

Taking his horse from the stables, he mounted it, offered me his hand, and I climbed on behind him.

"Why didn't Kitty come with you?" he asked. "She should have come to see me."

"She must remain at home. We're doing our best to find a house to rent."

"Rent?"

"Father is dead."

His face changed.

"I'm sorry."

"Thank you."

In his eyes was the fiery ambition that I was familiar with.

"I'll write to Kitty, but also you write to her as well. Tell her that if she will have me, I offer a courtship. I will come to Philadelphia to see her. And if all goes well, I will marry her."

Thus was the great release.

If there was one man that my sister deserved, it would be the Colonel.

"I'll hold you to it, Richard," I uttered. Mentioning his first name was not an unconscious thing. It was meant deliberately, indicating what Colonel Fitzwilliam knew all too well. I was accepting him as my potential brother-in-law.

He perceived and comprehended. We were of one mind now.

We rode through the streets.

Eventually we arrived at Pike's Stream and came upon the Tree of Human Souls. The willow was incredible to behold, and it was a true display of nature at its most ideal.

Colonel Fitzwilliam dismounted, then lowered me down and I removed a pocketknife from the pocket under my petticoat and apron.

"I'll be only about ten minutes," I informed him.

"I am in no hurry. It's nice to get out from the city occasionally."

He turned around, facing away from me and looking out, along the trees. Occasionally, he gave a side glance, to make certain that I was safe. Seeing him stand there, I grinned.

"What?" he asked, spotting my expression out of the corner of his eye.

"You can take the man out of the army, but you cannot take the army out of the man."

"Another habit that I cannot destroy," he remarked, "which I am happy for."

"I don't regret it. I need a guard right now." I began to chip away at the bark on the tree. "Do you ever regret it?" I asked.

"Regret what?"

"No longer being a colonel in His Majesty's army?"

I wasn't looking at the Colonel as I went about my work, but I sensed his deliberation.

"That is strange. I do miss the prestige of being a colonel, however, I do not miss the pressure."

"What pressure?"

"Of having to oversee men, as well as live up to an image. After all, as you know, I am not the firstborn. In England, I not only had very limited choices of profession that suited me, but I had to maintain the standard of my family. Also, father sent me to our plantations in Barbados. As you know, Lizzy, being a slave master never suited my palate."

"I know; I admired you for that." And I truly did. Colonel Fitzwilliam came from a family who made their fortune from the Trade, and from what he told me, he was the ONLY one in his family who found fault with that way of living.

"Thank you, but it's not admirable to know that wrong is wrong. It's just common sense. Well, I already disgraced my family with my abolition rants, but I was also fatigued from the constant image that I had to uphold. Money is important. Anyone is a fool to pretend that it is otherwise.

However, at home, it was always impressed on me that I had to marry an heiress. In England, I could never have married Kitty. But when I moved here, risking everything by putting all my savings into a tavern, it was the first time that I felt that I could remake myself. I didn't have to suffer under pretense, live up to that standard—I felt free. For better or worse, I felt free. I miss serving something larger than myself. But I have found purpose in other ways. And serving customers is infinitely preferable. This way, I make my fortune in a more constant way, and I get to meet people from all over the world."

I put some bark in my pocket.

"Dr. Warren has offered to take me on as an assistant," I said, "but I may need more work, because I might have to leave Lucas Lodge when I stay here."

"Why?"

I ignored the question.

"Is there any chance that you might need a scullery maid? I don't fear working after dinner and when others end their work-day. I have experience with working in taverns."

"The Lucases will find it scandalous to have you out so much?"

"Like I said, I might need to leave soon."

"Elizabeth, why?"

I had no choice now. Turning to Colonel Fitzwilliam, I didn't know what to do. I did not *fully* know his stance on what was happening in the world. If he was neutral to this all, I could rely on him. But it was hard to find out who to trust.

Then suddenly, a cold wind had come over me.

A crippling cold that had nothing to do with the weather.

It was as if a rush of ice had fallen upon my body and wind had rushed in around me.

Goosebumps crept along my skin, and I felt as if the air had become dense and stale.

I froze.

After all, I knew this sensation, for I had felt it all before, four years ago.

"Someone is coming," I uttered.

Colonel Fitzwilliam halted, his soldier-instincts took over and he froze as well.

"I don't hear anything," he replied, his ears perking up.

"I know," I assented, "however, I know it. Someone is coming."

Still with my hand on the tree trunk, and my knife in my hand, under the bark, I still didn't move. It was as if I had lost control over my limbs.

And then it came.

The sound of footsteps.

"Eliza," Colonel Fitzwilliam whispered, "don't move."

Colonel Fitzwilliam reached under his coat, placing his hand on the pistol that he had under his waist.

The footsteps came from a horse, but I knew that the mood belonged to the rider who was atop it.

I barely breathed, awaiting the inevitable to something that struck fear within my breasts.

But also, there was anticipation. A strange fascination with the dread that I was feeling.

I wanted this moment to last forever because I feared what would happen next.

But I also wanted time to move.

To face what I ought to have been prepared for.

The horse stopped, and then I heard a rider dismount.

Then, from among the trees, I saw a figure. I heard the underbrush snap from under his feet.

Suddenly, I did not want to remain passive under this moment.

Standing up, I put my knife away, with the bark still in my hand, and I moved around the tree trunk.

When I did so, I was faced with a man's back, who stood a few feet away, with his hand placed on the branch of a smaller tree.

He was wearing the familiar uniform of an influential officer in the British army.

When looking on his back, I saw his shoulders tense up.

The air and nature between us were awake and clearly warned him. That I was there.

Slowly, he turned around and faced me.

The first thing that I saw were his eyes.

His dark eyes indicated wonder, confusion, and a great deal of inner turmoil.

It had been four years since I saw him. But the face of the man who stood among the nine British officers who shot into the crowd at the massacre—it was his.

I was staring into the face of the man named Darcy.

CHAPTER 8

The Worst Way to Meet

An hour before...

L eaving the British headquarters, Darcy felt the need to see nature. Since he had grown up in Pemberley, Darcy always felt the urge for nature to call out to him.

He needed to see trees, rivers, and streams. The very confinement and closeness of things that clung to him when in town could be trying to his nerves. Also, his duties hung about his shoulders, and he just needed a release.

What could be said of Darcy was a desire to always be aware of his surroundings. When last he had been in Boston, he made a point to know of the best place, of the most ideal image of nature, and he recalled one Tree—a memorable willow that the Indians had named the Tree of Human Souls. A romantic name, to be sure. Yet, when he had finally rested his eyes on the tree, he could well understand the title.

First, the tree was regal, in every way, eclipsing many other natural elements that were around it. Truly, something about the tree felt not only relaxing, but familiar.

Though it was a willow, it had reminded him of an impressive tree that he used to run to when he was a child. It was near Lambton, by the Smithy shop. Darcy recalled the effect that its leaves and branches had on him, and it cast a spell. And such was the way with the Tree of Human Souls.

Although, it was more than that—there was something else wanting for explanation.

Something had seized Darcy so very suddenly. Yes, he always preferred to be among nature.

Indeed, rocks, tree, hills, and dales were more aligned with his natural intentions.

But that was not the true reason that he recalled Pike's Stream. The beauty of the tree called out to him, as if summoning him. He had been stricken with an impulse that this was the proper place for him to be.

When he arrived, he felt the comfort of the familiar. As he moved around, trying to encompass all in his sight, he stopped suddenly.

Hearing footsteps that were behind him, he tensed up, as that of a prey who knows a hunter is nearby.

But there was something about the sound that also made him anxious, but not in a fearful way. Rather, it was like that of anticipation.

This was something that he wanted.

'Turn around,' he told himself. 'This must be seen.'

With one foot in front of the other, he slowly turned around to face something that he never thought he'd see again.

A woman.

The woman.

Four years ago, he saw her face, and the memory was always forefront in his mind. It would drift in and out of focus, making it the only fascination that made him want to come to visit the colonies again.

So many days, weeks and months had passed, teaching him to suppress his fascination with a woman who was nothing more than a face amongst a bad experience.

And yet, here she was again.

In her eyes was wonder, alarm, and fascination. He rightly understood why and was wholly aware that he must have looked the same.

To know each other, and then not know each other. An antagonizing thing.

The man—he had returned to my company and my life!

An antagonizing thing.

Darcy, that is you. A British officer whose memory has haunted me for some time.

Immediately, the experience flashed before me of when he had to order his officers to shoot into the Boston mob. Of the pain in his eyes when he had to turn young men into killers. The alarm and fear that encompassed the scene, of their own colonists roaring at them, daring them into a fight. The heart-break in his eyes to know that their own countrymen were willing to overtake them.

Once more, pity rose to my breasts, and I felt sorry for him, only for it to immediately be replaced by wonder.

After all, there he was—again.

We both remained there, looking at each other for what felt like an eternity.

His eyes bore into mine.

And my disquiet filled up inside of his.

In those few seconds, our emotions flowed from without

ourselves and then filled up within each other, each having a mutuality to it. It was as if our thoughts had passed within each other, and then flowed all around us like a gust of wind.

I felt his anxiety.

He felt my astonishment.

I knew that he was scared.

He knew that I was worried about what would happen next.

He took one step forward—but that was not what released us from the purgatory of our confusion.

"Eliza!" Colonel Fitzwilliam called to me. "What is it?"

The spell was broken, and all the sounds that had disappeared from our attention had come rushing back in.

It was so loud. So terribly so as I came crashing into the small world that we had within ourselves, and between each other. I was mortified.

From around the tree, Colonel Fitzwilliam appeared. Quickly I turned to look between both men, feeling the sense of intrusion, but I was faced with more.

When seeing this Captain Darcy, Colonel Fitzwilliam stiffened and was aghast.

Captain Darcy's eyes narrowed, and if a human expression could hiss, his did. He was angry and enraged.

I looked back and forth between both men as they glared at each other, wondering what to do. Should I speak? Should I accost the situation? Then again, I had never learned much from standing around and letting miscommunication be the order of the day. In fact, whenever I let something go unspoken, from past experience, it never ended well.

"Gentlemen!" I snapped.

They both looked at me. Now all attention was on me. Brilliant! What was I to do next?

"Lovely," I asserted, "now we are getting somewhere."

I looked at Darcy, and for the first time ever, he opened his mouth to speak. I thought it best to help him on, in the best way that I knew how.

"Good day, sir," I began, curtsying, "I am Miss Elizabeth Bennet. Of the Pennsylvania Colony."

He closed his mouth and seemed at a loss of what to do next. Then he gathered his courage, and I awaited what he was about to say. I was filled with anticipation on what would happen.

"You," he said, his tone serious and his eyes dark with a subtle resentment, "you know my cousin."

First, I was filled with astonishment at the coincidence.

Secondly, I felt very much let down by the response. There was nothing to anticipate, nothing to wonder at. It was a question asked by way of a reproof.

I looked at Colonel Fitzwilliam.

"Cousin?" I repeated. "You are cousins?"

"You know him?" Colonel Fitzwilliam asked.

"No," I replied, "I've only seen him. As he has seen me." I looked at Darcy again. "Are you the man Darcy?"

He nodded curtly.

"We meet at last," I acknowledged, "and something tells me that this is not how either of us wished to begin it."

He nodded again.

I was growing impatient.

"Is that all that you have to say?" I asked.

"That's his usual way of reply, when he is angry," Colonel Fitzwilliam clarified, "but never fear, it's not you that he is angry with."

"Richard!" Darcy yelled.

"What!" Colonel Fitzwilliam replied. "You and I both know that you don't need to say anything for me to know. I can see it in your eyes."

"Yes, I suppose you can. We both were always quite good at reading each other."

Colonel Fitzwilliam removed his hat, running his hand through his hair, exasperated.

"Fitz," the Colonel said. "Let us calm ourselves and try and talk of this rationally."

"Rationally?" Darcy replied, stepping forward, his presence as intimidating as the Colonel's could be, when the Colonel *chose* to be. "What is it that I hear when coming? Is this all that you have to say to me? Your name is on reports. When did the name Richard Fitzwilliam ever align itself with the word 'traitor'!"

Colonel Fitzwilliam stepped forward, trying to shush Darcy.

"Cousin, please!" the Colonel declared, his tone equally as imposing. What I could say for the Colonel was that he was kindhearted, but never the sort to suffer being intimidated. "There is a woman present. Let me take her home and we can discuss this."

Darcy turned to me.

Despite that we had never officially met, I was aware of his mind, mentality, and mood. A quick succession of recollections swept through him.

He remembered when first seeing me at the Boston Massacre.

He saw me rush in to lament over the colonists who died.

And now he was seeing me with his cousin, in the woods. The bark in my hand may signify little, despite that it was obvious that we were not involved in any sort of romantic tryst. However, in times like these, sensibility can rush in, and one can lose one's rationality and give way to an irrational sense of resentment.

I admit that I was a little speechless as he bore down on me. This meeting was now marked as awkward, to say the least.

"You are cousins," I uttered, trying to distract him from where his thoughts were headed. "Do you not speak kindly to each other?"

Darcy did not reply, but stepped back, while still looking at me.

"Who are you to ask me that?" he asked. "What brings you before me now?"

I gestured to the bark.

"Medicine," I uttered. "I have an errand."

Darcy breathed out and in heavily.

"An errand?" he repeated. I perceived. He was repeating what I was saying, because he was trying to find his bearings. He did not know how to face me, because this was such a surprise to him. He was flummoxed. As well as myself.

"Yes. I have a friend who is ill."

"A friend?"

"Yes."

Out of the corner of my eye, Colonel Fitzwilliam looked in between us both.

"You said you never met," he wondered.

"No, we have not," I replied, still staring at Darcy. "We are strangers to each other."

When hearing me say 'strangers', Darcy's eyes altered from bewildered to decisive. I could not determine, nor figure why, but that word seemed to offend him. His posture straightened up, and I saw the captain in him return to his attitude.

"I should escort you back to your home," Darcy declared. "You can explain this to me."

"No explanation is needed," Colonel Fitzwilliam answered. "Miss Bennet is in my charge. It is wrong for me to hand the deed over to another."

Once more, both cousins glared at each other.

"A loyal British captain is infinitely preferable to anyone

with having the common fame of being treasonous," Darcy replied, his voice like ice.

"I know why you call me such," Colonel Fitzwilliam said. "But I've met many a dishonorable twat who wore that uniform. I no longer serve them."

Darcy was about to respond to this when I was at my wits' end. Naturally, it shall be learned of me that patience was not one of my chief virtues. Also, I had a distaste for conversations occurring in front of me, that were *about me*, that I had no part in.

"Are you both quite finished?" I snapped. "Because this conversation does not seem beneficial to either of you. You are like snapping turtles to each other, and not talking in a way of attempting to understand the other. Well, I have a sick patient on my hands, and I need to return. Captain," I said to Darcy, "I apologize if meeting me was uncomfortable for you."

"Uncomfortable for me?" he asked.

There he was again… repeating after me!

"I see it in your eyes," I replied, earnest again, "and I cannot explain it away. But what I can do is remove myself from this situation, so that you and the Colonel can speak freely." I looked at his cousin. "Colonel, please, escort me back to Lucas Lodge."

"I promised that I would, and I hold to it," Colonel Fitzwilliam assured me, offering me his arm. I took it. When seeing our arms link, Darcy's nostrils flared, and his scowl returned—if it ever left to begin with.

"Good day, sir," I said to Darcy. The Colonel and I walked away, with Darcy watching us as we walked along the underbrush.

"Cousin," Colonel Fitzwilliam said over his shoulder, "if you wish to speak to me, I still live where I always have."

"Is that all that you have to say to me?" Darcy replied.

"For the moment. Remember, there is a lady present."

Darcy turned away from us and stared ahead, at an invisible mark of duty that he had to set for himself.

"Of course. Your words have been marked."

Colonel Fitzwilliam led me to his horse, he mounted it, offered me his hand, I sat side-saddle behind him, and we were off.

As we rode away from the woods, I turned around, out of curiosity. I caught a glimpse of Darcy as he emerged from the trees, watched us as we left, and then went over to his horse.

"I think he might follow us," I whispered to Colonel Fitzwilliam.

"Oh, I know he will. And I know my cousin well."

I sighed.

Well, this meeting could not have gone any worse.

CHAPTER 9
The Follower

As we rode down State Street, Colonel Fitzwilliam had to slow down his horse, for safety. That gave me time to speak to him.

"Well," I began, "now is as good a time as any."

"Is it?" he asked. "For what, pray tell? Mind you, there are some things that are inadmissible to speak to a lady about."

"You really are going to be like that?" I asked, impatient. "Come now, Richard. I know the man you are. You despise not unfolding your true self. And you like talking to us women about what you really feel. I have two things to ask you."

"Very well," he gave in.

"First, you are among the Sons of Liberty."

I saw Colonel Fitzwilliam's jaw clench.

"It's better that you don't answer that," I accepted, "nor do I want you to. Never commit yourself in so open a way, and I respect that you do it properly."

When hearing me speak that way, his expression softened and he turned partly to me, while keeping his eye on the road.

"Again," I rushed out, "say nothing. These are dangerous times."

"But I must ask. What side do you fall on?"

"I am a woman. No one cares about my opinion."

"But you do have one?"

I grinned.

"Of course, I do. But how do I know if your heart is true? How do I know what side you fully fall on? How do I know that what I just saw was a scene you both performed, or if it was real?"

"Lizzy, you know that I don't lie."

"That's what a spy would say," I replied. "Colonel, we are friends. But only time will tell of what we can say to each other, regarding the situations that we are in."

Colonel Fitzwilliam smiled.

"Very good, Eliza. You must be cautious."

"Thank you for being proud of me." I shifted my focus on the more pressing thing. "And now, we can discuss a topic that I can get answers from. Your cousin."

"His name is Fitzwilliam Darcy."

I made a face.

"Fitzwilliam?" I repeated.

"Yes." Colonel Fitzwilliam chuckled. "It was done with the best intentions. He was named after his mother's family name, but as you can see—"

"What a terrible first name."

"I know! It works for a last name, but not a first one. He spent much of his life either being called Fitz, Will, or Darcy. He responds to all three, because his first name is an atrocity."

"An atrocity is not enough of a word for it," I replied, amused.

"You both have not met, but you still know him."

"He was there. At the Boston Massacre."

"Yes. He told me of what he had experienced there."

"While he was there, so was I. Mr. Lucas escorted me there

and I saw it all." My voice turned hollow as I recalled seeing the fray. "I saw the mob attack, and the British officers shoot into the crowd. I was worried about Crispus Attucks and George Hughes. When the smoke cleared, I ran among the chaos, and I found them both."

"They were already dead?" Richard asked.

"George survived, but Crispus was not so fortunate. I knew Crispus well. He should not have had to die like that. Not after working so hard to be free."

"I know."

"And your cousin saw it. He saw me weeping over them. We have known each other, without ever having the pleasure, or displeasure, of meeting."

"And now you saw him again."

"And again, not in the best of circumstances. Should we worry about him?"

"Not just him. Eliza, I have heard rumors. I cannot say much now, but my sources are reliable. Things are not going to get easier. But much might be worse to come. You see a redcoat, be wary, because they might be given orders that will have dire repercussions. The Boston Tea Party got the King's and Parliament's attention. And Boston will not go unpunished."

"I suspected as much. I will say this for the boycott; it was not violent."

"Precisely. That's what made the resistance admirable. We're trying to step away from any more acts of belligerence. But we can't always control our members."

"I know." I grunted. "That's what I am angry over. We let in the riffraff along with the principled. How can the world take any cause the colonists make as seriously if we show that we are animalistic?"

"There is no such thing as a revolution without there being

some savagery involved, on both sides. Believe me, this is common. No matter what we do. After all, the colonists spent years peacefully sending pleas to our Prime Minister, who ignored you all. Now the protestors have reached the end of their patience."

"What manner of man is Darcy?"

"He was recently elevated to the captain's chair. Like me, going into the army was the best option for him. We both are second sons. My father was Darcy's mother's brother. Darcy has an older brother, and two little sisters. Peter Jr, Georgiana, and Gretta. We went into the army together. We were very close as children and well into our teen years. For a time, I always assumed that resentment grew between us when I rose to the Colonel's chair quickly, but it was not so. Slowly, I had lost favor in my family, and in Darcy's eyes, when I was constantly talking about the abolition."

"The abolition?"

"Yes. I sympathize with their cause, and my family was tired of me always talking about it. Darcy especially."

My curiosity was awake, as well as my anger.

"Darcy's part of the family are slaveowners."

"Yes. Our entire family is. I was the only one against it, and they did not like that. Darcy found my ranting and ravings as that of betraying the family. As you can imagine, once I got the chance to retire from my commission and have the opportunity of buying taverns in Boston, I took it. I tired of my family looking at me like I was some sort of an abortion. And all of society, for that matter. In my opinion, many of them are as rotten as the African Kings who are always eager to sell their own people to us. Abolitionist societies are mostly in London, but my profession took me to all other parts of England that did not allow such openness of discussion. Our empire literally thrives because of the Trade, but we're not allowed to talk about it. Well, I would talk about it, and I lost popularity quite quickly."

"Poor you!" I declared, immediately sympathizing with him, and being angry with Darcy and the rest of his family. "In Philadelphia, it is like London. There, we can talk about it. But when my visits took me to other parts, and further South, it can be like what you describe as well. We're not allowed to talk about the abolition in those places. And your cousin joined the witch hunt against you?"

"Not as much with words or pitchforks, but he did lose respect for me. My cousin is aware that he can be resentful. His good opinion, when lost, is lost forever."

"He hates you for doing what was right."

"He was raised a certain way."

"You were raised the same way. So was my mother. Eventually, she felt the guilt of owning people. Therefore, it's hard for me to understand and sympathize."

"I see what you are feeling."

My anger was cemented. I went from accepting my curiosity for Captain Darcy to despising him. Life in the colonies had trained me not to be openly disdainful of slave-owners, and to treat them as any other. But I was a Pennsylvania abolitionist; we never fully kept our mouths shut. If I were to see Darcy, I would know how to react.

"Not being the eldest," Colonel Fitzwilliam continued, "Darcy lost his ability to oversee Pemberley."

"Pemberley?"

"That's his family's estate. It's one of the greatest houses in England and has one of the vastest grounds in the North. The Darcys are neither royalty nor knights. But they might as well be so, for Peter has the mayoralty of Derbyshire and is the local magistrate. But Darcy is the real leader, naturally more impressive, more decisive, and with a keen eye for business, overseeing his estates, and profits. Darcy naturally wanted to be the one to oversee the Pemberley grounds as well as making sure that their West Indies plantations were the most fruitful in the islands. But being the younger son, all he could do was suggest, and now was resigned to being in the military. And then I was promoted, which made sense. Darcy was more imposing, but I was more comfortable to soldiers, and I was given better reports. And then I was able to sell my seat and entered business. I wanted to make something of my own, and therefore, completed another dream that Darcy wanted: to run your own business."

"And then the resistance began," I noted.

"Yes, and then it began. Of that, we best not mention any more."

"No, we best not."

Eventually, we arrived at Lucas Lodge. Colonel Fitzwilliam dismounted and helped me down.

"Well," I said, "thank you, Colonel. This has been most interesting."

"Has it?"

"Of course. One of the most interesting afternoons that I have had in a while. And that includes when I was written out of the Quaker Meeting."

Colonel Fitzwilliam laughed.

"I am happy to have amused you. And that day that you were written out of the Meeting was an interesting story."

"Whenever someone gets kicked out of their religion, I suppose it always is amusing."

"Unless you were living during Tudor England, then it was not amusing," Colonel Fitzwilliam said.

"Or you were living in Salem during the Witch trials, then no, that was not amusing either."

I chuckled.

"Is it strange," I noted, "that the times we are living in are actually the better times?"

"Yes, I suppose so. That is very sad."

"So terribly sad!"

"I wish that I could call on you, but I doubt that the Lucases would have me. But still, give them my regards."

"Can I visit your tavern?"

He flinched.

"Women don't go to taverns without escort, but scullery maids."

"First, recall what I said earlier; I might need more work, so I might need your help. And second, yes, I am a woman, but I refuse to let that hold me down. You know that."

"Yes, I do. And you have experience working in taverns."

"Very much so. And remember," and here I lowered my voice, "it might be a matter of time before I am not welcome to Lucas Lodge either."

He did not reply, but his expression showed that he understood.

"Send a message by way of a servant, to let me know when you are coming."

"Thank you, Richard."

"You're welcome, Lizzy. Write to Kitty for me. I promise, I will not go back on my word."

"I know that you will not."

"Good fortune, Lizzy."

He egged his horse on and he was off, to the Green Dragon Tavern.

~

Now that I was alone on the street, I had time to reflect and gather my nerves before I entered the house.

With my hands on my hips, I breathed out and in, with my eyes closed. I did my best to calm down, refusing to allow any sort of anxiety on my face, so that I would not give myself away. I would tell Charlotte, by and by, but now was not the right time. There was too much risk involved, too much at stake. She was getting married, and it was her time.

As I opened my eyes again, about to enter the house, I felt the sensation again.

The tingly prickling in the air. All the goosebumps on my arms became more pronounced and the wind was filled with expectation and energy.

He was there! I knew it.

I turned around and looked down the street.

As I did so, wind picked up and leaves rolled around me, then rushed in the direction that I was looking.

As it moved the leaves and any garbage that was on the cobblestones along and away from where I stood, it brushed past a horse's legs that was a distance away from me.

Right next to a tannery and coffee house, the black stallion was impressive, as was the rider who sat atop it.

My eyes ran from the stallion's hooves to Captain Darcy, who sat atop his horse with a regal and majestic position.

He had followed us. As I had suspected.

And now, I felt the fear rise within me. I had assumed that he would follow Richard Fitzwilliam, but not care to know where I was. After all, both men had much to discuss.

But that was not so.

Now, he knew where I lived. And I was living with loyalists.

But since he knew my past, I had been compromised, and the Lucases could be guilty by association.

Now I felt guilt. What had I brought them into, by mere association with me?

Although that was only one of my worries.

Darcy *now knew where* I lived.

Easily, he could learn of my movements, have me followed, and quickly discovered how deeply were my patriotic sympathies.

I was being watched.

But, within me was the resilience of finding a way, no matter what. And then I fell away from my woes when I investigated Darcy's face.

I knew him and marked him.

He was looking at me in wonder, but also, I was as much a mystery to him as he was to me. I felt the scene widen around him, his horse became ominous, and his presence grew larger than life.

He was just a man. However, something else was going on that was—for lack of a better way of phrasing—of a strange phenomenon. I was worried that it was some sort of evil spirit that had risen from the earth to envelop our acquaintance, but I dismissed it.

I merely attributed it to a strange and religious link that we had been forced to have forged between us from the experience that we had underwent from the Boston Massacre. We both experienced the tragedy of that event—and so it linked us.

That was the best way that I could explain what was occurring.

But there he was, his eyes intense and his expression set. And I returned the gaze.

It was now determined. We would see each other again. And again.

Sighing, I tore my eyes away from him, knocked on the door and the servant, Gretchen, opened the door to me.

Quickly, I rushed in, but did not give Darcy a backwards glance, hoping not to encourage him.

I thanked Gretchen and took off my market wallet as I went to the kitchen to begin to mix the medicine.

Suddenly, I felt restrained and confined. It was as if my body was rebelling against the clothing that I was wearing. Walking past the cook, I removed my mobcap and let my hair fall down my back.

"Miss Bennet?" the cook asked. "You are looking flushed."

"I can well believe it," I replied, "never fear, Jessica. This is just a passing thing."

I began to make the medicine and doing my best to release Darcy from my thoughts, but it was proving most difficult.

"Can you tell Charlotte that I am here?" I asked.

"Yes, miss."

Jessica left and soon Charlotte came in, hastily.

"Lizzy," Charlotte said. "I saw you come home from the window. Was that Colonel Fitzwilliam that you rode home with?"

"Yes, it was," I admitted.

Lowering her voice, Charlotte dismissed Jessica, and came up to me.

"Lizzy, you must be careful. We have heard news of him. There is talk that he sympathizes with traitors."

"He was being kind and rode me home from the Tree of Human Souls. I had to get bark for Maria's pain."

"Very well. I respect that, for he is chivalrous, but you must lessen your company with him. Don't let him being from England confuse you. My reports might be correct."

I closed my eyes. I truly did not wish to confess this now, but Charlotte was my friend.

Looking into her beautiful face, I suppose that it could no longer be concealed.

"Whether he is or not, is not my concern," I said, "because of a truth that I must impart you with."

Charlotte's eyes shifted, wary.

"What truth? What must you tell me?"

I sighed again.

"Charlotte, we are friends. And no matter what, I will always admire you, and think you are a brilliant woman. I hope, after this all is said and done, that you can still respect me."

Charlotte was no fool. Compiled with her beauty, was a sharp intelligence and vast ability for deduction. Jane, Kitty, and I were fortunate to have not been born under a jealous star, because not only was Charlotte vastly superior to us in looks, but also in mind.

When I spoke, Charlotte did not need to wait for me to explain. Her eyes were filled with alarm, she moved away from me, shuddered for a bit, went to the fireplace, and leaned her arm against the top of it.

"Lizzy," she extoled, resigned, "whatever you are about to say, say it quickly."

I lowered the bark and the kitchen mallet that crushed it down. Then I tucked my mobcap into my pocket under my petticoat.

"Charlotte," I began, "I did not intend for this. But I cannot help myself."

"Lizzy, we can all help ourselves, with what we believe. You know this better than anyone when you rebelled from your Quaker beliefs."

"Not beliefs, but practices."

"Either way, I know the woman you are."

"Yes, you do. Therefore, please try to understand."

"Then tell me quickly! And be done with it."

"I am a patriot."

Charlotte continued to look away from me, but I saw the despair in her eyes.

"I know that I ought to be sorry, but I am not," I said. "I rebel against these oppressive taxes without representation. I rebel against us having no rights and being regarded as inferior. I never changed my mind, and still hold to it. I am a patriot."

Now I had said it.

This was where it would all get harder.

CHAPTER 10

The Next Act of Defense

Over the next couple of days, Captain Darcy found himself extremely busy with the arrival of more British troops that were coming in through Boston Harbor. This gave him ample time to avoid having to face his rabblerouser of a cousin, and to briefly forget Miss Bennet.

Of course, neither person was far from his thoughts, and he was stricken with a dual desire. With his cousin, nothing could garner much joy in speaking to him, but that of a favorite cousin of his, who he had to constantly chastise.

Even after all their arguments and disagreements, Darcy never forgot when he once admired Colonel Fitzwilliam. The envy of his military position was once keenly felt, but Darcy understood why eventually. After all, Colonel Fitzwilliam was older than he was, as well as more experienced at commanding officers. When Darcy had enlisted, he was rather green, whereas Richard was already brown. Also, Colonel Fitzwilliam was charming, which naturally helped him pave the way for his future. Jealousy had transferred to admiration, then that admiration had transferred to confusion, and that confusion to anger when Colonel Fitzwilliam had lost his mind, sold his commission, and went to the colonies for no reason. And then he dared to scoff at the Darcy and Fitzwilliam families' chief means of obtaining income.

The cousin that he once admired now assumed that he was better than the rest of the family.

Therefore, talking to Colonel Fitzwilliam could bring Darcy nothing but disappointment.

And yet, all of that was trivial when knowing if he would meet Miss Bennet again. Sadly, he hadn't fully remembered her first name, but he knew where she was visiting, at Lucas Lodge.

However, what was agonizing was that he also knew how that situation would unravel. Like it was with Colonel Fitzwilliam, meeting her again could bring him nothing but misery. Every time they had encountered each other, it had been a disagreeable experience.

And yet, he still desired to see her, to speak to her, despite that the longing would always be let down by when it eventually happened. There was no way that seeing her would live up to all the expectations, all the desire to learn more of this woman who dwelled in his thoughts.

But there was nothing for it.

Although, in this rare instance, Darcy had the ability to be too preoccupied to let his emotions pray on him. If he had been a gentleman, then he would have been idle, and it would have forced him to dwell on these occurrences. However, between the movement of armies, and the anxiety of trying to gain more spies in New England to infiltrate secret organizations and learn more of what was going on, Darcy was able to fill up his time and only think of Miss Bennet when he was retired for bed.

That morning, as his batman was helping him dress, there was a knock on his door.

"Enter," Darcy replied, "I am decent."

The door opened and Sergeant Bingley walked in, seeing

that his captain was already wearing his white breeches, smock, and waistcoat. Then the batman put on Darcy's frock coat, with an old-fashioned small standing collar, with white coat linings, which had a blue patch at the front with a gold button and embroidered loop. His buttonholes were placed in pairs. This was the traditional uniform for a lieutenant-general, but it suited a captain's attire as well.

When entering, Bingley took one look at himself, and immediately was ashamed. This did not go above Darcy's notice.

When facing the Sergeant, Darcy had no choice but to inspect his uniform. Sadly, it was lacking in one respect.

"Sergeant," Darcy stated as his batman was making sure no hair was on his coat, "you know that I am like you, and prefer to not wear a powdered wig when in service. I am not a hypocrite and will not chastise you for that. However, your waistcoat and breeches are buff. Now, they are supposed to be white."

"Aye, captain," Bingley responded, a little apprehensive. "If it was convenient, I would have a new pair of white apparel, but due to the strain of uniforms in the colonies, there is little distribution. My uniform is a little outdated."

"It's not your fault, then. Hopefully, with this new shipment arriving today, it will have fresh supplies."

"I could purchase some items from a local seamstress."

"You know Colonel Forster's orders; we do not purchase our uniforms from any dressers in the colonies. It puts a strain on us, I am aware. Yet, this is part of the political reprimand to New England."

"Do you think seamstresses took part in the dumping of the tea?" Bingley joked.

"Not a jot, but rules shall be rules. Without them, we plunge into chaos. But with these colonists, chaos seems to be their preferred way of being. You know me, Bingley. Do not speak casually if you have business to report."

"Yes. Forgive me, Captain."

"I am not upset. It's your habit to be social. Now, continue man."

"I just wished to inform you that Governor Gage is going to be arriving in an hour." Bingley looked at himself. "And I will not have white breeches by then."

Darcy half-chuckled.

"As you were."

"Thank you, sir."

As Bingley turned to leave, Darcy had a thought.

"Bingley?"

"Yes, sir?"

Darcy did not speak immediately, but Bingley had learned to give his captain time to ask certain things.

"Have you—what do you think of these colonists?"

"Which ones?" Bingley asked.

Darcy raised an eyebrow.

"Are you intentionally trying to be dense?"

"No, Captain. Indeed, I am in earnest. It's very hard to meet two colonists who are precisely the same. Do you want to speak of the loyal ones, the traitorous ones, or the indifferent ones?"

"Good point."

"Besides," Bingley stated, "I am not paid to have an opinion. And I enjoy that."

"Do you?"

"I do my duty."

"Everyone has the right to have an opinion."

Bingley smirked.

"Try being a sergeant sometime."

Pause.

Suddenly, Darcy laughed.

"Well," Darcy said, "that was good enough for a laugh."

"Thank you, sir. I feel as if I have accomplished something now."

~

An hour later, Darcy had prepared for General Gage's arrival.

He stood outside, with Bingley and his officers behind him. The cook had prepared everything, the servants had cleaned the entire headquarters, and everything was fit for the governor.

Eventually, the royal governor arrived in his carriage, with his guards following him, and Darcy was able to finally face him.

General Gage had recently become the military governor of Massachusetts, and Darcy was of the impression that the promotion may have been flattering but was not easy on one's health.

Despite that Gage had recently returned from Weymouth further down the Bostonian shores because he needed a brief holiday to help his health and see a doctor there, Gage was still recovering from exhaustion and ailment. He was a man in his mid-fifties, was of medium height and weight, and he also did not wear a wig. He had long and thick gray hair, that he had tied back with a black ribbon.

When seeing Darcy, his attitude shifted from a fatigue to alertness. Darcy's spirits lifted when he saw Gage immediately shift to professionalism and was prepared to like him.

"Governor Gage," Darcy said, "Captain Darcy, I report to duty under you."

"At ease, Captain," Gage said.

Darcy lowered his salute but remained with perfect posture as he escorted General Gage inside.

"And as my captain," Gage continued, "you may call me general instead. I am more accustomed to that title."

"Thank you, General. I was briefed on your favorite dishes, and the cook has prepared it for you. Also, time has taught me that generals are not always very keen on immediately tending to their duties on arrival and need a brief while to rest."

"While I would find rest infinitely preferable," Gage replied as he removed his tricorn hat, "I do you a discredit for leaving you ignorant of my orders and what I have requested from Parliament. When in Weymouth, most of my hopes and expectations have been answered."

"Expectations?"

Darcy dismissed Bingley, and followed Gage into the inner chambers, where they could discuss matters privately.

Gage sat behind the main desk. Darcy informed his batman to tell the cook to prepare the meal, and both men spoke of strategy in the meantime.

When Gage sat down, Darcy remained standing before him, his posture and face painfully standing at attention.

Gage sighed.

"Captain, did I not say that you can stand at ease? Take a seat, man."

Darcy sat down, but his posture was still painfully straight.

This led to General Gage chuckling.

After the general's laughter died down, the batman announced that food was prepared.

"We'll eat in here," Gage replied, his tone returning to serious.

The food was brought in, and Gage began to eat. Darcy declined, acknowledging that he was not entirely hungry.

"But I do thirst for knowledge, general," Darcy began. "What news from Parliament? And what actions are being taken to respond to the Tea Party?"

"All in good time," Gage responded, eating. "All in good time."

Darcy leaned back and watched Gage eat his food.

Either he was really hungry, or he was not moved to stand on ceremony. He ate very greedily, taking large bites, and sometimes the juice from the food dripped down his lips and trickled down his chin.

Secretly, Darcy was repulsed. But he did not flinch and only concentrated on the sloppy eating habits of his general.

Basing his opinions on first impressions, General Gage seemed like a walking contradiction. Darcy was still undecided on whether or not Gage was a man that he would like or dislike. He was trustworthy, that was certain. But Darcy was the sort who never fully felt comfort with any of his superiors. He never acquired the best skill at it. Time would tell between them all.

As Gage neared the end of his meal, he wiped his mouth.

"Captain, which regiment will you oversee?" Gage asked Darcy. "I was not briefed on your station."

"I'm the captain of the 16th Light Calvary. I requested that station, as opposed to the Heavy."

"Why not the Heavy?"

"Light Calvary are light dragoons, who are elite officers who specialize in their weapon handling and horsemanship. Soldiers of light calvary are in the British army out of choice. As opposed to being pressed. I prefer to captain over men who prefer to be in the service, as opposed to men who were forced to."

"A wise reason, but we have to press men into service," Gage said, "or Britain would not have the standing army that it does. But I can comprehend your intentions."

Gage rubbed his eyes, leaning forward and focusing. In his eye was a sudden ferocity.

"Astounding, is it not?" he asked Darcy. "That it has come to this?"

"I—"

"You don't need to answer the question. Who knows what could possess these villains who stand against us?" Gage turned to Darcy. "I prefer to have my officers be aware of the man that I am. Were you briefed on my history in the colonies?"

"Very much so, General," Darcy replied, happy that he knew how to answer the question. "You came to the Colonies in 1754, at the beginning of the Seven Years War. You participated in General Braddock's campaign in Pennsylvania."

"That disastrous beginning of my career."

"It was his fault, not yours. But then you transformed yourself when you financed the first Light Calvary regiment in 1758. You eventually were made governor of Montreal in Canada. Next you became Commander-and-chief of all British forces in North America. It was the most important post in the colonies."

"And I maintained it through order in handling matters of diplomacy, communications, Indian relations, and boundaries along the west. All of that, all of my service to these lands, and it has come to this."

His eyes were filled with fury.

"Ungrateful wretches!" he hissed. "These disgusting traitors have been screaming at us since 1761."

"1761?" Darcy asked, surprised at this. "That long ago?"

"Yes. It's often forgotten that the first protest against British Laws was James Otis oration against the Writs of Assistance that was passed. People forget, but I remember. That's when the seed of poison began to create so many weeds that we now have infecting our colonies." Gage wiped his lips. "The Sons of

Liberty are a cancer that must be removed from all of New England."

Darcy looked at his lap, recalling his cousin, the Colonel. And Miss Bennet.

"I've heard that it's your letters to Parliament that have made them aware of the problem throughout the years," Darcy furthered.

"Yes. I have done my best to make them aware of the horrors that I have constantly come across. The worst of them is Paul Revere, John Hancock, and the main villain is Samuel Adams."

"Samuel Adams. Shocking that he is John Adam's cousin."

"Yes."

"The same John Adams that defended our soldiers during the Boston Massacre."

"Yes. But don't let that one act of defense fool you. My informants have told me that John Adams still has sympathies toward the rebellion and will not stand by the British during this crisis."

"But at least he does not encourage violent acts, like Samuel."

"True. But he will not stand with us, to be sure." Gage's face became resentful. "You were wise to return to England during this time. I've seen it all. The slow growing of a viper in our bosom. I made certain that Parliament and the King knew of the dangers, and how we had to be decisive in our attack on these fools.

The Sons of Liberty formed in the summer of 1765. Like spiders, they thrived and spun their web. In that summer, the Boston Sons marched through the streets and burned an effigy of Oliver. He was one of the taxpayers that enforced the Stamp Act on the colonists. Then they broke into his house and looted it, rebelling against the tax. When the chief justice Thomas

Hutchinson refused to renounce the tax, they looted and destroyed his house as well. But that was not the end of it. After Parliament passed the Townshend Acts in 1767, Samuel Adams organized a boycott to keep British goods out of Massachusetts altogether. The Boston Sons sent boys to smash windows and smear excrement on walls of local shops that did not fall in line with them. It was the worst kind of harassment, and they do this under the guise of liberty. And if that did not scare the shop owners, the Sons would possibly kidnap them and tar and feather them."

When hearing this, Darcy was angry, to say the least.

"How many people suffered from this villainy?" he asked Gage.

"Enough. And I intend to meet fire with fire, as I have done before. I thought bringing more troops into Boston would frighten them off, but like an evil nest, they are thriving. And I will burn everything. I did not remain in these colonies to lose control over them now. Parliament has guaranteed and accepted my suggestions. It's called the Coercive Acts."

When hearing that, Darcy felt his chest rise with excitement at the idea of knowing that more decisive measures would be taken to put the colonists in their place.

"What will the acts entail?" Darcy asked. "I was briefed on these measures before, but I would like to know everything."

"The main one will be the Boston Port Bill. It will close down the port of Boston, and it will not reopen until the Bostonians pay us for the tea that they destroyed. They also accepted my proposal to invoke a Quartering Act. We shall move British officers into any private home, to show these people that we will leave no stone uncovered and we will make their lives hell until they submit. Among these terms are the Massachusetts Government Act. Colonial Democratic institutions will be stripped of their power and will be superseded by the British military government."

"Quick and decisive. A good strategy," Darcy approved.

"I am happy that you approve. Also, I must inform you now that you will remain a captain, but we are a little thin on the ground when it comes to brigadier-generals. You might have to be called upon to do both duties until I have sufficient staff. Never fear, you shall be known to fill both posts, given your experience on the battlefield."

Darcy put aside his previous indecision about Gage and was determined to like him. He was promoting him, but still keeping him where his talents were best in. Also, Gage was not passive or attempting to understand the colonists' grievances. He was hard, firm, and he knew how to bend them to submission. With Gage, Darcy was certain that he had a general that would put an end to this infernal rebellion and soon, all the Boston Sons would be brought to justice, and sentenced.

"When shall we enforce these acts?" Darcy asked.

"I got the permission this month, but they will not be enforced until June," Gage responded. "That gives us time to prepare, arrange curfews, and have enough British troops on the street to meet any resistance. The question then becomes for us to choose which homes to have British officers settle in. I want them to be in every neighborhood in Boston, and set up officers in the countryside, to monitor who comes in and out of Boston. I want homes that I know will be spacious enough for the officers and will be comfortable enough for them."

"I have a home to suggest," Darcy blurted out.

This caught Gage's attention. He leaned forward in his chair and faced the captain.

"Which home?"

Darcy flinched at his own rashness.

Suddenly, he cursed his impulsiveness, angry that he had done what he had done. In his desire to be acute, a good officer, he also put a woman in danger, when that was not his intent. But it was also done out of selfishness, and he needed to answer.

"A home," Darcy extolled, "that goes by the name of Lucas Lodge."

CHAPTER 11

Correspondence

Walking to the post office, I managed to cross paths with Lugeon again and his grin was as memorable as ever. Memorable in the sense that half his teeth were gone.

"Poor man!" I said to him. "If you survived to be sixty, you either would have no more teeth left, and someone has to mash up your food for you, or if you come into money, you will have to buy dentures, and those would be painful."

"I've never seen dentures, so I would be none the wiser."

"Oh, it is hard!" I exclaimed, asking the post clerk if there were any letters from Lucas Lodge, bearing the last name Elizabeth Bennet. "You have to clamp them down onto your jaw. It's agony."

"Who would put themselves through that sort of hell?"

I grinned.

"Politicians. Obviously."

The clerk came back to me, announcing that there were letters with me as the recipient, but he was hesitant to release them to me.

"Never you mind, miss," he said, "and I do not wish to be offending you, but I cannot hand you the letters."

"Ah," I replied, not surprised. "You fear the prospect of handing letters to someone who is not who they say that they are."

"Precisely. You understand me."

"Fortunately, I have my birth certificate with me, and I always keep other letters on me, and receipts of payment that I have from other employers."

Lugeon grinned.

"You've done this before, haven't you?"

"Sometimes the only way to keep a secret is to go directly to the source," I responded, taking items from out of my market wallet. "And letters can get intercepted too often or gone astray. Sometimes, one must take matters into their own hands."

"It's dangerous to bring one's birth certificate around," the clerk said.

"I've made many mistakes, sir," I replied, "enough to no longer make mistakes like losing things."

I showed him the items, and he reluctantly gave in.

"Very well," he said, "if I give in, the quicker that you will leave."

"I appreciate your apathy," I retorted, unwilling to look any other way than to be amused. This is a trick that I learned; if you pretend to be unphased by someone's cruelty, it only makes them angrier. Life is interesting in that way.

I took the letters that were given to me and began to look them over. I had six letters, and they were equally exciting to hear about.

One was from my sister, Jane Bennet. Habit had trained me to know that it was from Kitty as well. They both wrote their letters together, to save paper.

The next letter was from a wealthy acquaintance of mine, Elizabeth Drinker.

Another was from Mary Ludwig Hays, a woman that I rarely saw, but we had remained friendly through our constant correspondence. The next letter was from another friend of mine, an Irishwoman named Lydia Darragh.

The fifth was from another friend, Margaret Cochran Corbin. She was living in Western Pennsylvania.

"Surprising that her letter arrived around the same time as the others," I commented. "The west part of Pennsylvania always can be hard to correspond with."

The next letter was on the wrong side, so I had to flip it over and I was surprised.

"Betsy!"

The last one was from a friend and fellow ex-Quaker like myself, Betsy Ross.

~

"You look like the wind has been knocked out of you," Lugeon commented.

"I have good reason for it," I replied. "Betsy only writes to me when there is something wrong. It's strange, because in person, she is quite optimistic in nature."

I thanked the clerk and turned to Lugeon.

"Keep the remaining teeth in your mouth," I said, by way of a farewell. "Mashed up food is not pleasant."

"Who can control one's teeth?" He called up to me.

"Rub them with rags," I said, "wash them down with brandy or any strong alcohol, and clean in between each tooth with some sort of pick. Food gets caught in between teeth, and that's how the rot begins."

"Do you fancy yourself a dentist?" he asked.

I opened the door.

"No, I'm just passing through."

I left the post office and walked down the street. As I turned the corner, there was a tavern nearby. In front of it was the hold which horses were tied to, while the men were inside.

Going up to the horses, I patted one of their heads and stroked its hair.

"Please, don't mind if I use you for a place to lean on, will you?"

Turning around, I leaned against one of the horses, and he didn't move.

"I must feel like nothing, eh?" I asked it as I removed the first letter from my wallet.

Opening it, the first one was from Jane.

Dear Lizzy,

Kitty and I have finished all arrangements, and our father's home has not been currently bought yet. However, when we must leave our home, we have prospects of renting lodgings on Second and Chestnut Street. It is still quite close to all of our acquaintances, and Kitty and I have our employment. I still can run an apothecary shop there.

I cannot write more because Kitty wishes to share this paper with me. I miss you terribly, and please write a response as soon as possible so that I am aware that you are safe and have arrived in Boston well.

Lizzy, for me, do your best to leave your political opinions to yourself. I do not want you to fall into trouble in Boston. It's not the city you are from, and you might not find any shelter from harshness there.

Lizzy, it's Kitty now. Well, you fortunate soul! I know not to worry over you, because you know how to survive travels.

Well, I have no choice but to be brief. How are the Lucases? Is Charlotte as disgustingly beautiful as ever? Never fear, I speak in jest. You know that jealousy is something I overcame toward her, long ago.

We have heard a great deal about what is going on in Boston, and I am not like Jane. I am starved to know. Tell me everything if you can. I have learned not to trust newspapers, because not all reports are accurate.

What are the British planning? Are the Sons of Liberty on the move? What will the retaliation be?

Even here in Pennsylvania, there is worry about what is happening in New England, and we are becoming very aware that this conflict will spread. We worry over the poor people of Boston, and what they will soon suffer. Also, I have gotten work as a scullery maid in Munn's Tavern. The tavernkeeper, Samuel Nicholas, was willing to take me on.

Talks of boycotts are everywhere. Mark my words, this will not end soon.

Tell us what is happening.

Love,
Kitty

Love,
Jane

Ps – Tell Charlotte that we are very happy for her.

I closed the letter and smiled.

Next, I took out the next letter, and began to read Mary Ludwig Hay's letter. She wrote mostly about married life and trying to maintain during this time, but there was one passage that struck out to me. It was about her sympathies, and her husband's, William.

... and onto other matters. Let us know all that is going on. For you are there, and the journalists in this colony only get their words from other sources. YOUR import will be fact.

And it's not just I that am starved for information. William wants to know all as well. He knows that Britain's response to the Tea Party will be extreme. And he is prepared for that. Dr. William Irvine in Carlisle is beginning to assist in boycotting the Tea Act. William has his support, and other men are joining.

Eliza, you know that I follow William wherever he goes. But even if not so, I think—Elizabeth, there are whispers of Independence. Of the idea of liberty. What do you feel?

I find... the prospect is frightening. And yet, I know that the very concept of independence is also intriguing. There is an electricity about all things when people's passions are stirred.

That's the problem with whispers of liberty, or rebellion, if you will. It starts, and it cannot be hushed up so easily.

But I do find the idea of fighting for what one believes to be—of interest.

I know where you stand. I do understand what you are feeling. I think—that I might feel it as well.

When closing the letter, I felt a whirlwind of sensations. Mary was correct. There were frightening times ahead. But Mary was like me; she had her courage. And it did not belong solely to her husband.

Speaking of independent intentions belonging not only to her husband, I opened the letter from Margaret Cochran Corbin.

As I read, my heart was amused, because Margaret's personality always was present in her writing:

Oi', you Scottish Pennsylvanian rogue, you! Tramping to New England, where all the action is. Kitty wrote to me of how the Quakers cast you out. Well, that's their mistake!

Believe me, Lizzy, you're better off than those old bores. You know how I respect Quakers, but sometimes, action requires to be met with an equal and opposite retaliation. Something my parents would have taught me, if they would have been given the time.

Well, you know the way the wind blows with John and me. Steadfast to the end. John is considering joining the Pennsylvania Militia, if the fight decides to come further down to the rest of us.

I told him that it might not come to that, but with more British soldiers coming into Boston, as you wrote me, then who knows?

But I tell you this, if a fight is upon us, John and I will not duck. You know me, Lizzy. I was not given this red hair for nothing!

Ha!

Etc.

MCC

Ah, that is so like Margaret!

Removing the next letter, it was the reverse. I sighed, willing to brook the powers of disagreement. After all, different viewpoints did *not* an enemy make.

Opening the letter from Elizabeth Drinker, I began to read. She spoke of her family, who was ill, and angry at me for not being there to help nurse them—and then slyly praising Kitty and Jane for their medicinal abilities… I knew that she was doing it to be spiteful toward me. Even Quakers were not without human flaws to them.

And then, it came to what it always came to. I was in Boston, at the center of where much of the conflict was beginning. She could not help but express her worries as well. And here is where our differences began:

> My dear Henry and I just read the paper this morning about the news of more British officers entering Boston.
>
> Lizzy, I want you to promise me that you will not go flailing your beliefs about. You bring no help to your family by being outspoken. Besides, we ladies are not meant to be so very bold.
>
> And why do I tell you this? After all, I know that, no matter what I say, you will always go your own way. Please, friend, know that I do it to protect you and wish that you return home safely. You know that I do not judge you for what happened last year. Our practices can be hard to live by, and our codes are strict. I like that structure, but it must have gotten too confining for you.
>
> But I pride myself on holding to our values of non-violence and remaining out of any conflict. If this tension does rise between us and Mother Britain, I cannot follow you. I admire you, dear friend, but I will take no side. Neither will Henry,

and our family. You walk down a path that I cannot share.

You will always be welcome in our home. But not your beliefs.

I still respect you, Lizzy. Never forget that.

Etc.

ED

When lowering the letter, I was not surprised again by her words. I knew what Elizabeth Drinker, and her husband Henry, were devoted to. They were Quakers to the last; they would refrain from taking any side in this conflict.

I understood why. And it made perfect sense to me. Conflict is like anything. Both sides cause a mess. A great mess, and it gets to the point of being confused about who is right and who is not. Does this surprise you to know? I might have my sympathies, but it does not destroy my ability to be objective. It is something that I pride myself on, more than anything: the ability to see everything clearly. I knew what I was about. And what others were about.

I was about to open the last letter when I was interrupted by a couple of slave women being chastised by their master. It led to quite the to-do, and I moved forward to see the master's wife beginning to slap one of the slaves after she dropped one of the baskets.

"For god sakes, miss!" I cried. "She did it by accident. Let the girl alone!"

The mistress and master wielded on me with a fury.

"Who the devil are you to interfere?" the master asked.

"A woman," I replied, "did you not care to notice?"

"Our property is our property," the mistress argued, coming up to me, "mind your own business!"

I arched my eyebrow.

"You both are my business. You are causing a raucous and are attacking your fellow women. If you are going to accept the evil role of owning someone, at least do it with some kindness. And don't give them the edge of your evil. And if your evil looks meant to frighten me, then you are terrible at it. You couldn't frighten me if your lives depended on it."

I walked up to the slave women and offered them my hand to help them up, which they took.

I turned back to the husband and wife.

"And if you plan to attack me when my back is turned, I am tougher than I appear. Also, I'm a stranger, passing through. Good luck trying to ruin my reputation. You will fail because there is no one to cry to."

Not caring to be in their presence, I walked away from the conflict, pocketed Betsy Ross's letter again and decided to not read it till I got closer to Lucas Lodge.

For the love of Socrates!

Why must there always be something to ruin a perfectly good day?

As I arrived at Lucas Lodge, I was faced with a shocking sight.

There were a few horses in the front, all majestic in look. The riders were not present, but there were two guards at the front.

And they wore the redcoats that belonged to his majesty's service.

My heart turned cold.

What had I brought to Lucas Lodge?

CHAPTER 12
The Intolerable Act

I stood there, as if I had been rooted to the spot. Immediately, I felt guilt rise within me and I was struck by the awareness that the Lucases would be ruined by their mere association with me. What a shocking blow it was! To think that I had prided myself on my ability to disappear into the crowd, that my sympathies toward one cause would remain hidden.

After all, I was a nobody.

A woman of no consequence.

In fact, being a woman rendered me to be almost invisible under the great weight of influence. Rather than view that as a disability, I had used it as a strength. After all, what was rendered invisible, could make it easy to be overlooked.

Had I misjudged that ability?

After all these thoughts swirled around my mind, making me feel instantly defeated, I knew that I could not remain where I was.

This was, either way, my fault. I had brought crisis to my friends' home, on Charlotte's special time.

I would not let this suffering to pass. Whatever would

happen, I would be the only one to endure the consequences of my loyalties. But one thing was certain. I had to hide my letters.

Before I was seen, I ducked into an alley by Tettle's China and houseware shop. Quickly, I put the letters into the pocket under my petticoat and made myself decent.

Gathering my courage, I walked up to the house and was immediately ordered to halt.

"I am a guest here," I explained. "My name is Elizabeth Bennet. If you were to send for Sir William and Lady Lucas, or Henry or Charlotte, they shall confirm that I visit them."

The officers stood up straight and erect.

"I have been given strict orders to inspect the contents of any person who was to visit, while Captain Darcy is speaking with Sir William Lucas."

My eyes widened, and I immediately began to feel the deep and dark pain in my stomach. Once more, the wind began to sweep under my feet, and the tingling of expectation began to rise.

"Darcy?" I hissed.

"Aye, Miss."

Darcy had given the order to come to Lucas Lodge. Suddenly, I was filled with anger, a burning resentment that led to me removing my cloak and thrusting my market wallet and haversack bag in the officers' hands.

"Search it quickly," I ordered. "And take me to your captain."

Both officers were unnerved at my bold speech. Honestly, I was not surprised. I was sure that when I was no longer in their company, they would have a great deal to say about me.

Finally, I was admitted, and I prepared for the worst. But one thing was certain; the Lucas family would not suffer for this.

When I entered, I was met with the Lucas women that were sitting in the main parlor.

"Lizzy!" Charlotte said, rushing up to me. "You will never believe what has happened."

"The British officers have decided to set up housing in this residence?" I asked them.

Charlotte looked disheartened when she realized that I was already aware of the situation.

"Sorry," I acknowledged, "did you want to tell me?"

"Yes, I did. Now I am vexed that I could not deliver such news."

"How is Maria?" I asked her and Lady Lucas.

"On the mend, fortunately," Lady Lucas said. "Lizzy, there will be a sudden change to our household. Four British officers are going to set up their quarters in Lucas Lodge." She approached me and held my hands. "I am so sorry, but you are going to have to give up your guestroom and sleep with Charlotte. Our two guest bedrooms must be given to the redcoats."

"Four soldiers!" I blurted out, aggravated. "That's four more mouths to feed!"

"Lizzy, you must lower your voice."

Although I knew it was best, I was a little hot-tempered, and was not in the mood to suppress my feelings.

"This is the lowest that I can go when I am annoyed," I replied. "Having four soldiers living here. That will be a great financial strain on you all."

"It's not for us to object," Charlotte replied. "This is our duty. Besides," and here she lowered her voice, with guilt in her eyes. "This is the traitors' faults. We are being punished for their actions."

I ground my teeth, becoming defensive.

"What the revolutionaries have done does not warrant this, and is not my fault," I whispered to her, so no one could hear.

"I know it's not," she whispered in reply. "I am just speaking the truth. We are being punished for their sins, and you know it."

I sighed.

She had a point. Between the tea being thrown overboard the three ships, the constant boycotts that were happening, and the sadly too frequent tar and feathering going on, retaliation was to be expected. But here, it was being placed in the wrong direction. Here, the wrong people were being punished.

"I do not understand," I stated. "You all are loyal to the King. You are known Tories."

When saying that, the effect was immediate. Lady Lucas flinched, and Charlotte bit her lip. My slip of the tongue did not go unnoticed.

"We are loyalists, as we ought to be," Lady Lucas stated. "Lizzy, the term 'Tories' is a derogatory phrase that we are called. You would do best not to use it."

"Forgive me," I replied. "That was my fault. But the fact remains that the British are making a mistake for quartering officers in this house. Or in any house, for that matter."

We were interrupted by a person clearing their throat.

Turning around, it was a redcoat, and judging by his uniform, it must have been an officer of the light calvary. He was in campaign dress, with a redcoat that was a cut-down version, an undress coat with white lace instead of gold and no epaulettes. He did retain his sash and gorget. His uniform was impressive, but he was not a man of much power.

"Is there any trouble?" he asked.

"No," Charlotte rushed out calmly. "All is well."

"Really?" He turned to me. "I thought I heard raised voices."

"You did," I replied simply. "As the guest to this house, I have the liberty to speak, independent of the rest of the people in this residence. And my words should not be their blame, but my own. I object to the occupation of this house."

"Not being a resident of this house, you have no right to speak."

"On the contrary," I said, walking up to him and staring him squarely in the face. "I have every right. And if you are to be uncivil enough not to address me like a lady, then I can refrain from viewing you as a gentleman."

When seeing me refuse to humble myself, the reverse happened. Instead, the man removed his hat, embarrassed.

"Yes, quite right, I am in error."

He bowed to me.

"Sergeant Charles Bingley, at your service, Miss."

I grinned. When I was a child, my mother told me a saying: most people fear when you get too close to them. Once you do, they lose the bark to their bite. And the more manners that they were taught, the easier they are to unnerve.

Mother, you had never been more correct.

"Thank you, sergeant," I replied, curtsying. "Now that is better. And I have no choice but to respect you."

He smiled, and I was amazed to know that his expression was genuine. If I were to judge things by first impressions, I would determine that he was the sort of man who had a natural kindness to him, or simply wanted to be liked. But not in a vain sort of way. Time would tell.

"Well, I agree to that," Sergeant Bingley spoke, his shoulders slackened, and he was more at ease. "It's always preferable to be respected."

"Well, you appear to be disposed to have an openness of mind, and I appreciate that."

"Thank you, Miss."

"Bennet. Elizabeth Bennet. I am from Philadelphia, the Pennsylvania Colony."

"Oh!" he exclaimed. "I have heard of your great city. It is said to be one of the best places in the colonies."

"Thank you, sir."

"You are welcome. I do wish to go. I wished to have gone, at this point, but my situation has made it impossible."

"I understand. And thank you for being kind."

"No thanks needed. You are correct. You are a lady, and I ought to be more courteous."

For a moment, I felt a slight change of my preferences. Was I wrong to not ally myself with the British? There were men like this Bingley man in every regiment. Would it be so wrong to remember such characters?

In the next second, my mind returned to its original declarations. I had seen the good and bad of the regulars, of all the wrong choices being made, of when the British would attack whenever we protested. Of us Colonists always being regarded as unequal to those born on British soil. And if we did not do something about it, we would always be regarded as such. We had to make them listen. We were equal.

"If all officers and the King were like you, Sergeant," I acknowledged, "I think I would be apt to like you all."

He chuckled, his cheeks red.

"Well, Miss Bennet, this is too much praise."

"Actually, it's an apology, because of what is about to happen next."

Bingley looked down at me, confused.

"What is about to happen next?" he asked.

"Might I ask where Captain Darcy is?"

"In the library, talking with Sir William Lucas and his son."

"Good."

"I still don't understand what is about to happen."

I gave him a determined look.

"This."

I shifted to the right, the left, back to the right, and then I darted past him, running down the hallway.

"Wait!" Bingley cried, running behind me, "Miss Bennet! Wait!"

I reached the library's door, knocked on it quickly, said 'forgive the intrusion', and then I yanked the door open.

All three men were sitting down, and their bodies jerked in astonishment as they turned to me.

Sir William.

Henry Lucas.

And standing up was Captain Fitzwilliam Darcy.

Gathering my courage, I was prepared for the worst reaction to my entrance.

"Elizabeth!" Sir William muttered, alarmed. "You are intruding!" His face shifted when he assumed the worst. "Good God, is it Maria? Has her sickness worsened again?"

"Maria will live, I promise," I replied, even though there was no certainty of it. My attention was seized by Captain Darcy's presence.

When seeing him, the familiar haunted feeling fell between us, and it broke upon our attention like a strong wave upon the shore. When seeing me, his eyes were also unmoving.

Unafraid, I returned his gaze. Whatever was between us, there was no point in pretending that it was ineffective. Denial to a reality could only carry you so far before you had to accept the contrary.

"Then what has brought you to impose yourself?" he asked. "Begging your pardon, but we gentlemen are speaking of business."

"Lizzy," Henry said, wary and worried about me, "it is best to return to the ladies."

"I apologize for my intrusion," I said, amazed how I was still talking when I was so much affected by Darcy's presence. "But there is an urgent matter which I must discuss with Captain Darcy." Still looking him in the eye, I was indicating that I was not going to leave until I received satisfaction. Only then did I realize that Sergeant Bingley was standing behind me.

"Forgive me, Captain," Bingley rushed out, "I did not anticipate the situation and I have been in error."

"It's not his fault," I overrode him. "Forced entry, and I was faster than the sergeant. I humbly ask that you pardon him." I took a few steps forward. "Captain, I request an audience. I want to believe that you will not turn me away."

Darcy's jaw dropped open and his thoughts were written across his eyes. Despite the transparency, it was not needed. I knew the confusion etched in his emotions. He wanted to speak alone with me, posthaste.

Although, he also wished to keep protocol and dismiss me and talk only with the men.

These conflicted desires danced across his powers of decision. However, we did not have all the time in the world. And nor did I, for that matter.

"Captain," I asserted, "what say you?"

CHAPTER 13

The Bridge & Wall Between Us

A t last, Darcy opened his mouth.

"Sir William," Darcy ordered, "your guest and I are acquainted, and there is a particular question that I must ask her."

Sir William was apt to agree, but Henry had a natural apprehension about the matter.

"Father," Henry objected, "it might be best if I remain behind as Lizzy's chaperone."

"Thank you, Henry," I said, grateful. "I appreciate your concern, but I shall be well. I know that the good captain here will not be satisfied until he knows the sort of person I am."

Sir William and Henry looked confused, and I could well understand why. After Charlotte accepted that I was a patriot colonist, she swore that she would not tell anyone else in the family.

Captain Darcy, however, had never had a full conversation with me, and yet he knew more about me than they did. That was most unsettling.

The state of unsettlement was not reduced to me, but to Darcy as well. Like me, he knew that he would not be satisfied until we had gotten the chance to speak. And that could only be achieved by us being alone.

"Despite the indecorous and inappropriate request," Darcy stated, "your guest is correct. I need to be given more of an explanation of Miss Bennet's role in this household."

Despite Henry's reaction, the men had no choice but to comply.

"I shall wait in the parlor, Lizzy," Henry Lucas whispered to me.

"Thank you," I replied, happy to know that I still had him for an ally. "Remain close."

He nodded and we were left alone, except for Bingley.

"Shall I stand watch outside of the door?" Bingley asked.

"I am not going to hurt him," I remarked over my shoulder. Bingley chuckled.

"Leave us," Darcy declared.

At last, we were alone.

After all this time, after all these years, and now we would speak to each other.

"Your sergeant is a good man," I replied.

"Yes, he is. And rallying quite well for a widower in mourning."

"He lost his wife?"

"Yes," Darcy answered. "When I first met him, hard drink was his best way of recovering. But now he is better."

Well, this was a strange beginning.

"Mr. Lucas," Darcy began.

"Sir William?"

"No, his son."

"Henry?"

"Yes." Darcy's eyes narrowed. "He seems to worry over you. Is it affection?"

I raised an eyebrow.

"That is a bold thing to ask, and not much to the purpose of what ought to be discussed. However, if it will satisfy your curiosity, no, we are not attached. I have no means, or inclination, to chain the Lucas family down to being no more than a family that I have befriended."

This time, it was Darcy's eyebrow to lift.

"What does that mean?"

"I think you know." I threw my cloak down onto the chair nearby and stood near the fireplace. "Captain Darcy, whatever is happening here, is wrong. And as a captain, a man of honor, I ask you to remove your officers from this house and give them no quarter here."

"You ask that of me? But by the way you speak, you make it seem like it was a command."

"If I had the power to order you all, then it would be. However, I do not have the authority. You do. And I want to believe that you know that you have committed a wrong here. The Lucas family are loyalist colonists. To quarter officers here, is punishing them for what other Bostonians and New England patriots have done."

"Don't use that word."

"What word?"

"Patriot," he sneered. "These villains are not patriots. They are traitors and violent mobs."

"You know as well as I do that both sides have committed violence and injustice. Therefore, I call them as they feel themselves to be." There was a personal slice in my tone. After all, he had insulted me, however ignorant he might have been of it. "But that is neither the point nor reason for why we speak now."

"Is it not?" Darcy asked.

I sighed, resigned.

"Oh, very well," I gave in. "Let us not beat around the proverbial mulberry bush. Whatever assumptions that you have made of me gives you no right to take it out on these people."

"Assumptions? Are you about to argue about what I think of you? Is it not fact?"

"These are struggling times, trying times, and confusing times. I have no problem admitting that I understand both sides of this situation. However, this moment is not about what I think of you, and what you think of me. Am I wrong? Did you not choose this house because you saw me enter it after your cousin escorted me home? It's not right to quarter redcoats and your officers to a house of people who are already loyal to you. Do you not see that this does not help those who are true to Britain? You only make more enemies. This is an intolerable act."

Darcy's eyes turned dark.

"You have quite the nerve in calling something intolerable!"

"Do I?" I asked, unafraid. "Go on, Captain, humor me." I sat down on the other side of the desk. "What was that declaration for?"

"Miss Bennet, the first time I see you, you run through a riot to hold onto dead bodies who deserved what they got."

"Some of them were a violent mob, I do not deny. But with Crispus Attucks, he had reason to be angry at all the British soldiers tyrannizing Boston, and reason to show it."

"What you call tyrannizing," he replied, defensively, "was not so, but was us restoring order to chaos and anarchy!"

"I can understand the impulse to regard it as such," I said. "I will not take that from you. The Boston Massacre was wrong and was mob rule in every way. But I also know what I know. Violence had been rallying between British officer and colonist since 1770. The Massacre was the culmination of all those frustrations, be it right or wrong."

"It was wrong. But you admit that the massacre was wrong?"

"I admit it freely."

When hearing that, Darcy's eyes shifted from defensive to calm. Then his eyes began to twinkle. He was happy that I agreed with him. That also brought some joy to me as well. The moment of agreement passed between us, and I felt my skin feel as if there was an inner light. I could not deny that it was the contentment that radiated from him, and it was being projected onto me.

How hard it is to keep sense about oneself during such times.

"But again," I stressed, "I know what I know."

"And what do you know?"

"That this conflict has brought out the villain on both sides, and that is the way of a fight. Our methods of violence are not correct, but that was after years of us trying to speak to you and plead for the same rights that those have on British soil. After all, *we* are British. Now violence has broken out, and *now* you notice us. How can it be concluded that you are outraged at such vehement actions, when those actions were the only way that those rebels could get your attention? Also, you do not regard us as equal."

"Equal to what?"

"To those who are from the mother country. We expect that, when we meet each other, you understand that we are British subjects as well, and that we ought to be given the same regard and respect as those from actual Britain. But we are not regarded as equal. We are considered inferior to you. From Parliament's refusal to give us representation in the government, to the King constantly disregarding us. It's almost as if you consider us not to be equal to you all."

"Well, you are our colonies."

I groaned inwardly.

"And what does that mean, Captain?"

"Well, you are inferior to us."

When hearing that, I grew as still as a statue. Whenever I was offended, that was usually my method of being. Standing still, feeling nothing, but looking as if I was preparing to find my revenge later.

There was silence between us, where Darcy and I only looked at each other.

My eyes were fire.

His were stone.

But even stone cracks under a certain level of flames.

Eventually, Darcy tore his eyes from mine and looked down at his lap. Huzzah! I would take my victories wherever I could find them.

"Miss Bennet, what I meant was—"

"Oh, I know *precisely* what you meant. You were honest with me, and you said precisely what I have already known. Now I thank you."

His brow furrowed.

"For what?"

"For giving me reason to despise you, captain."

"Despise me?"

"Yes. I do despise you now. Surely you must understand why."

Darcy was a little unnerved and I was very aware of why. I did not speak my last sentences with venom, but in casual tones. Sometimes a way of showing one's feelings is indirectly. My tone was not harsh, but light and easy. While also being sincere.

"I have offended you," Darcy acknowledged, "I see that now."

"Yes. You did. But, like I said, it was nothing that I did not already know. If you confirmed this, then my beliefs are a certainty. You look at me, a colonist, and think that I am inferior to you. A person born and raised on the British island. You have given me reason to feel a sharper clarity of what I feel. And how I ought to see this situation. I owe *you* for this clarity."

"Miss Bennet—"

"There is no use canvasing this argument," I interrupted him. "For that is not what the point of this meeting is, nor is it what should concern either of us."

"Then what do you want?"

"To talk about this quartering in Lucas Lodge." Putting aside my pride, I abandoned all selfishness. "I came to Boston because Charlotte is my friend, who is getting married. I was invited here to attend the event. This family is devoted to the Empire, supports King George, and has been open to paying any tax, despite the retaliation for paying them. Always they have been faithful to our Mother England. Do not do this, captain. Do not make their lives difficult. If you did so, due to their affiliation with me, then you hurt the wrong people. I am not in the mindset to have others suffer because they know me. Also, if this was done for other motives—motives such as knowing my whereabouts, then you can set your heart at rest. I am leaving this house."

Darcy leaned forward, aghast.

"Leaving? Are you returning to your home?"

"No. I do not have the money to pay for the journey. As such, I have gained employment. Once I have enough income, and have watched my friend wed, then I will book passage on a ship back home."

"A ship?" he asked, his eyes lit up.

"Yes."

He placed a finger to his lips, considering something. I sensed that there was something he knew that he was not telling me.

"What is that face for?" I asked.

"What face? This is my normal face."

"No, it's not. You are being shrewd now."

"It's nothing of your concern."

"And I do not believe you."

Darcy tapped the desk with his hand, a little vexed.

"What are you?"

"Elizabeth Bennet."

"No, I just… what sort of woman are you?"

"I'm a Pennsylvanian woman. I take it that you have never met the likes of me before."

Darcy did not respond.

"No need to answer," I asserted. "I can interpret your silence."

"Pennsylvania?"

"Yes. And a half-Scottish one."

His eyes grew more alert again.

"You're half-Scottish."

"My mother. She was from Aberdeen." I rolled my head, amused. "Now I know what that look on your face is for."

Quickly, he tried to mask his expression, but I knew that look. I knew it all too well.

"I do not think anything," he replied.

"Yes, you do. It's too late, Captain. I know what you are feeling, and I know how to prepare myself for the future. Your face showed everything of what you think of me. And of the woman who bore me."

"It depends how your mother would have regarded individuals such as me."

"I think she would have analyzed you properly. My mother had a way of knowing what people were like. As do I. Now, let us return to the subject. I am leaving this house. And when I do, do not follow me. Leave me alone. And this family."

"First," Darcy said, taking a step toward me. "You are wrong, Miss Bennet, to assume that I have the authority to remove the officers from this house. The order was done by General Gage."

"Gage?" I said, wincing. "The same General Gage who was made the lead of the military in the colonies?"

"Yes."

"Why? He has no affiliation with this family."

"But Lucas Lodge is a strategic place to hold officers and meetings. It's a spacious home, of a respectable look. A little shabby for my tastes."

"This home is lovely!"

"Not compared to mine. If you were to see my estate, you would know."

"Yes, I daresay that I would," I said, and my tone was like ice. "Considering how the house is supported—and who suffers to pay for that house."

Darcy's eyes shifted. He was no fool. He knew that I was judging his family's way of receiving income.

"Now," I concluded, going to the door, "I ask you this, captain. Regardless of my animosity for you, and your belief in my inferiority, I ask you to advise Gage that quartering in Loyalist homes will not enhance British support in Boston, but only add to its opposition. You have nothing to gain by this. Leave this house, Captain, for all your sakes."

I opened the door.

"Miss Bennet!" he cried, moving closer to me, and shutting the door in front of me. I did not look at him but remained looking at the door. I would not give him the satisfaction.

"Yes?" I asked, still staring at the door. However, I was aware of his close proximity to me.

"I do not want you to leave this house on my account."

"You misinterpret, Captain. Ever since I realized that I was causing a hindrance here, I knew that I was a harm. I had already planned to leave. Never fear, I shall be out of your life, and you will not have this inferior colonist to blight your view."

"You are content to be angry with me forever?"

"Did you not notice till now?" I asked, finally turning to him.

That was the mistake.

His face was so close to mine that I felt the intensity of his intentions. And he felt my emotions drifting from the surface of my skin and melting into his. It did not matter now, how hard that I showed my contempt of him. The link was there again, and now it was stronger than ever. I should have left while I could.

"I don't believe you," he said. "I do not believe that you hate me. I think you are angry that I was rude before and that you take great pleasure in taking on prejudices that are not your own."

"How dare you?" I questioned. "To think that I do not know my own mind. Well, I do."

He pressed his hand against the door, to keep it closed.

"Let go of the door, captain."

"Not yet."

"Do so, or I will scream and say that you would not let me leave."

"You would not."

"Why would I not?"

"Because you are too proud to."

How did he know that? Of course! My emotions were in my eyes.

"Point taken. But you are being vulgar."

"I am being nothing that you have not awakened in this conversation. Miss Bennet, how do you know my cousin?"

"The Colonel?"

Now his expression changed to something more sinful.

"I saw him with you, alone, in the woods. Miss Bennet, I deserve an explanation."

"He was my chaperone when I was getting bark from the tree. For medicine."

"That is what you would have me believe?" he asked, skeptical.

"It is the truth. What you believe is your own affair." And once again, that sinful look flashed across his face. "You are jealous."

"I am not."

"Yes, you are. Do not deny it. Either way, there is nothing to worry over. Colonel Fitzwilliam is my friend. And he is engaged to my sister."

"Your sister? He is?"

"As of a few hours ago, yes, he is."

He was temporarily relieved, and then he returned to being defensive.

"Miss Bennet, you must sever your ties to my cousin. He is dangerous to be around now."

"I do not abandon my friends, sir. That is not my way."

"You will be in danger just by being affiliated with him."

"He is your cousin; are you not also in danger just by being affiliated with him? Now, let go of the door."

Darcy had no choice but to agree, and I opened it.

"Tell General Gage my advice," I said, "but have it come from yourself. Let him see reason. And farewell, Captain Darcy. Hopefully, we shall never have to see each other again, but for when I have to retrieve my items."

"Where do you go?"

"To find rooms to let while I am here."

And with that, I left him.

As I rushed out of the door, wrapping my cloak around my shoulders, Charlotte came after me.

"Lizzy, where do you go?"

"To leave this place." I looked at her sympathetically. "Charlotte, there is no need to worry. This has nothing to do with me, as it turns out. But I cannot stay here. I shall return by nightfall."

With that, I left.

CHAPTER 14
Dark Water

O nce I left Lucas Lodge, I made my way to Doctor Warren's home. Doing my best to appear nonchalant and unsuspecting, I always looked behind me to ensure that I was not being followed. I took a very public, but indirect route, that made it hard to follow me.

However, there were many British regulars patrolling the street, but they took very little notice of me. I was stopped only once, and when I answered that I was going straight to the doctor, to get a second opinion on a sick friend who lived at Lucas Lodge, I was allowed to continue my way. Within ranks, news traveled fast of where British officers were remaining.

Despite that, I had to keep my wits about me as I walked, for I could not help myself as my mind also was filled with the previous events.

The morning had begun so well, and with so much promise of peace.

And then it all had unraveled so horribly.

Lucas Lodge now would host British officers, who would move in there, eating and drinking whatever they wanted and paid no money at the Lucas's expense.

While Darcy was not ultimately responsible for such a choice being made, I still could not deny that I wondered if he was not secretly enjoying this.

What was General Gage thinking? Did he believe that having his officers set up in a home would be agreeable? That it would assist his cause?

At last, for the first time, Captain Darcy and I finally met. And it was awful. Truly, it could not have gone any worse, and with each leaving the one with not only more questions, but more contempt.

For my part, I had no regrets. Darcy was insufferable and possessed all the self-importance that I could imagine belonged to a pompous British officer, inflated of his own pride, of being a man of the English aristocracy. And why ought I have been surprised? Such repulsive behavior always resulted in such characters who reaped the rewards of a lovely upbringing that was brought about by the suffering of others.

How unlike he was to Colonel Fitzwilliam in every way!

And yet, why? Why did this strange connection exist between us that was altogether provocative and disruptive? Nothing good could come of us interacting with the other. He thought himself better than me, not to my surprise. My life was filled with meeting characters such as him before, and I would not be set down by the tedium of those sorts.

But whatever mutual respect we both could have had for each other, was now over. He had ruined it in every single way. He had given me an excuse to not know him. To not care to understand him. He was unfair and unjust.

Before I knew it, I was standing in front of Dr. Warren's door.

I had arrived without even knowing it. Truly, my mind had been wandering without any hint of getting lost or getting myself lost. My feet knew where they were heading, even if my head was somewhere else entirely.

I knocked on the door and entered.

∾

When I entered, I was met with a surprising trio of individuals.

I turned to see three men face me.

Naturally, the first was Doctor Warren.

The second was Alexander MacDougall, Charlotte Lucas's fiancé.

And the third was Samuel Adams... the man who had arranged the Boston Tea Party, the most influential man when it came to arranging getting Bostonians to boycott buying British goods, one of the founders of the Sons of Liberty—and also the cousin to John Adams.

∾

When I had entered, all three men had stopped talking and had turned to me.

"Miss Bennet," Dr. Warren said, with a forced smoothness that gave all the indication of them having to recover from a secret discussion.

That was the sad truth of these three men; they were not good at being deceptive. Their eyes said everything.

"Good day, Dr. Warren," I replied, but my attention was just as seized by the second man. In between the three men was Alexander. "MacDougall, man, what brings you here?"

"Lizzy," Alexander responded, putting his tricorn hat on, and walking up to me with a haversack bag slung over his shoulder. He fastened it quickly, and it didn't escape my notice.

"I was just passing through and I decided to inquire about Maria and see how he was getting on in assisting her."

"Well, the best way is to see her yourself."

"You know that I do not want to always be at Lucas Lodge," Alexander responded, smiling as he flashed his surprisingly good teeth. "You know that I've got a bonny lass of a fiancée, but I do not want to annoy her family by always being there."

"I do not think that they would mind," I said, and then I had an idea to verify my suspicions. "Although the British officers who now live there might disagree with you."

When hearing that, his casual tones transformed to one of rage. As I knew it would.

"What!"

"Yes, I just came from there. General Gage has exercised his authority and has stationed four British officers to take quarters at Lucas Lodge, for free."

He walked up to me, angry.

"He did not!"

"Lex, he did."

"English tyrants!"

He moved to leave, and I knew him well. He was about to do something drastic, and I knew that was the last thing that the Lucas family needed.

"Lex!" I declared, taking his arm. "Do not go there yet. Not until you calmed yourself."

"It's the ultimate disrespect. Are we to have no rights or say or anything?"

And once more, he confirmed something that I now was learning about him. Something that would shake the very foundations of Charlotte Lucas's future.

"All that I know," I stressed, "is that if you go there, you will make trouble for the family. Visit tomorrow. Lex, please, tell me that you will listen to what I say."

He bit his lip, looked behind me and at the windows.

"It's more than that," he uttered. "I've got word from my family in Scotland."

"You have?" I asked. "What does that mean?"

Suddenly, he remembered himself and realized that he had let too much slip out.

"Never you mind," he replied smoothly, trying to encourage me to forget his declarations. "Lizzy, you know me. I rattle off and then speak a lot of rubbish in the end. I'm always talking away about much of nothing."

Well, there was nothing for it but to be let down. Whatever door that he accidentally opened, would now be closed.

"Indeed."

"You are right on the mark about one thing," Alex said. "I have business at home now anyway. When going back to Lucas Lodge, tell Charlotte that I'll ramble along there tomorrow."

"Aye, laddie," I said, attempting to do a thick Scottish accent like his. I failed at it horribly, but it only led to us laughing. And then he left.

Gathering my courage, I turned back to Samuel Adams and Dr. Warren.

"Well, Joseph," Samuel Adams said, pretending to have asked about a proscription. "Are you sure that this arsenic will help my headaches?"

"Yes, it will," Dr. Warren replied, "but take it when you are eating and only the proscribed amount. Too much might not be beneficial."

"Too right, too right."

There was no vial of arsenic, so I must have been led to believe that it was in his pocket. Samuel Adams and I had never met before, but I knew his face. Therefore, I suppose it was only natural for him to assume that I was not wise enough to discover his lie. He never came for medicine.

"Well," I said, "I offer you good luck with that headache. They can be painful and distracting ailments."

Samuel Adams turned to Dr. Warren.

"This is Miss Elizabeth Bennet," Dr. Warren said, "my new assistant."

"Assistant?" Samuel asked, surprised. "Well, Dr. Warren, this is quite the surprise."

"I can assure you, Mr. Adams," I asserted, "that I am experienced in such matters, and I will do my duty well."

Hearing me talk in so bold a way also astonished Mr. Adams.

"Oh, well, it is just that a lady—"

"To be a lady is like being a man, Mr. Adams; it is not a disability. It's a calling."

Well, now! Mr. Adams, the legendary revolutionary, and even he did not know what to make of me.

Since I felt like I was losing in every respect, in all other directions, I would take my victories where I would again.

"Well then," Mr. Adams said, dismissing me and turning to Warren. "I do not agree with such speech, and—"

"And this is my practice," Warren said with finality. "Get along with you, Samuel."

Samuel Adams gave a slightly indignant look, as if he was about to say something cruel, but then he thought better of it.

"I am being rude, aren't I?" he asked us both.

"Yes," Warren and I said, accidentally in unison.

"Well now, never mind, I can see when I am being licked," Samuel Adams admitted. "Even I can be wrong sometimes."

'And other times,' I whispered in my thoughts.

Adams bid his farewell and left.

When we were alone, I turned to Dr. Warren.

"So that is Samuel Adams?" I asked.

"Yes," Dr. Warren said, with a twinkle in his eye. "Now that you have met him, what do you think of him?"

"I would say that it is too early to tell, but I also do believe in first impressions," I acknowledged, believing all my initial assessments—assessments that have often proven to be true. "And I do believe that he is the sort of man that you can like one moment, and then dislike in the next."

Dr. Warren chuckled.

"Elizabeth, you are very good at studying character."

"One of my few achievements." I smiled, but I knew that I was on a schedule. As such, I had to be economical with my time. "I know that I am an hour early."

"Yes, you are. How do you account for being too punctual?"

"Because I need your recommendations. I came here because I need to know if there are any lodgings that I can rent in the area, that accepts weekly lodgers?"

He looked at me quizzically.

"Whatever for? Are you not staying at Lucas Lodge?"

"I cause a danger by staying there."

"A danger?"

I rolled my lip in between my teeth, shifting my tone. Now was the time to not let my courage slip away from me. After all, there was nothing to fear.

"Joseph," I said, intentionally using his first name. "What I am about to say is something that I do not wish for you to respond. In fact, if I am right, always stay silent. That is enough."

I went to the window and closed the curtains, so that we

could go unnoticed. This quietly alarmed Dr. Warren, but he did not move.

After closing the curtain, I moved to the fireplace, that was the furthest from the window, and looked into the fire.

"I know that you are among the Sons of Liberty," I said.

I was met with silence.

"But what I must know, and again, do not say anything, is about Alexander MacDougall. Is he a member? Is he a patriot?"

Again, I was met with silence.

And that was enough.

Sad now, I sat down in a nearby chair. Rubbing my forehead, I was trying to ease the trouble that was beginning to give me a headache.

"Oh, dear lord." I sighed. "Charlotte is among a loyalist family and is now marrying a man who is secretly a patriot. This is going to end awfully."

As I sat there, I still saw how Dr. Warren barely moved.

"Well, it is confirmed," I said. "Lex is like us."

"Us?" Dr. Warren repeated, shifting in his place. He took a few steps to the right, circling me unconsciously. "I cannot imagine what you mean."

"That's good," I replied. "In times like this, it is better to be cautious and not give anything away. I can assure you that we have the same sympathies. I am no spy or here to compromise you. However, still stay cautious. No one has ever achieved anything by being upfront and public in such a way. Yet hopefully this next acknowledgement will help you learn to trust me. I have to leave Lucas Lodge, because by order of General Gage, British officers have taken quarters there. It's altogether nonsensical."

"Nonsensical in every way!" Warren declared. "As well as being counterproductive to their cause. What can they gain by that?"

"There, you see?" I stressed. "My being there can bring the Lucas family nothing but by terrible association. I will not tear them down. I need to leave their house immediately."

"I understand. While I will neither confirm anything that you suspect of me—and I never shall—go to the Green Dragon."

"The Green Dragon? Colonel Fitzwilliam's tavern?"

"Yes. From what he has told me, he rents out two rooms upstairs, and the lodger left the residence two weeks ago. The rooms should be open."

"When is the soonest that the Colonel shall expect rent to be paid?"

Dr. Warren went to his desk, took out twelve shillings and handed them to me.

I looked at his hand. It was strange, seeing it there. Those shillings were all that I needed. But I did not take the money at first.

Then I sighed, angry at having to owe someone.

"I am tired of having to come to you for everything," I admitted. "It is getting vexing for us both."

"Will it make it easier if I take it out of your wages?"

Now I could breathe. I took the money.

"That is more agreeable."

Jumping up, I made for the door. Stricken with immense gratitude, I turned around, ran up to Dr. Warren and I embraced him. My arms wrapped around his waist surprised him, but he only chuckled and tapped my arms.

"Very well. Get along with you, and hurry back. Mr. Jenkins had an accident, and the infection has made his leg go gangrene, and it has to be amputated. I need your assistance. So, return quickly."

"Never fear, I am not afraid of running in the streets."

"I know that you are not." Dr. Warren laughed. "Do not fatigue yourself, though."

"Right."

I left his house and immediately headed for the Green Dragon.

Happiness filled my spirit as I realized that everything was working out well.

I felt a little bit of guilt because I did not tell Dr. Warren everything of what I intended. I just needed a little more time to find out how I was going to tell him the news.

CHAPTER 15

The Color Green

W hen I arrived at the Green Dragon tavern, there
was a horse tied up in the front, and I recognized
the stallion and the saddle.

Walking up to it, I ran my hands along its mane
and patted its nose.

"Good afternoon, Briseis," I said to the horse. "I had no
idea that my cousin was here. But perhaps it is better that way.
Like it or not, he knows where I stand on things."

I walked into the tavern and was immediately met by
surprised looks. After all, ladies did not go to taverns unless
they were escorted by gentlemen, and I was alone.

Behind the counter, Colonel Fitzwilliam was filling mugs of
ale and brandy, with scullery maids going back and forth,
tending to customers.

"Miss Bennet," Colonel Fitzwilliam asked, inviting. "Well,
this is a surprise."

"I can well believe so," Mr. Collins said. I turned to where I
heard his voice and saw that he was sitting in a corner with a
few other men. "And so am I. Any chance you are looking
for me?"

170

"I come with a different purpose, but this way, I get to kill two birds with one stone," I said. "I need to talk with you."

"Of course, you do."

"Do not go anywhere, rascal."

"I've got a few minutes before I return to the tannery. If you dawdle too long, it's not my fault if you miss me."

"Never fear, I come with a point."

I walked up to the counter and addressed the Colonel.

"Dr. Warren told me that you have two rooms upstairs for rent."

When hearing this, the Colonel squinted, his interest piqued.

"Yes, I do."

"Have you found a new lodger for it?" I asked. "Sorry that I talk so quickly, but I have to walk back to an amputation in an hour. I can make rent. If you are willing to take me on, how soon can I move in?"

Colonel Fitzwilliam leaned closer to me, and he could see the panic or urgency in my eyes.

"Tomorrow. Rent is three shillings a week."

"Excellent. I can make payment. And when it is time for me to leave the place, I will always give you a week's notice. How soon can I see the rooms?"

Colonel Fitzwilliam looked past me.

"Margaret?" he said to one of the scullery maids. "I might have a new tenant. Escort Miss Bennet to the rooms upstairs so she may inspect them."

"Very good, sir," Margaret responded, taking the key that the Colonel gave her. "Right this way, miss."

As I followed her to the steps, I passed Mr. Collins.

"Do not leave," I insisted, tapping him on the shoulder.

"That depends on how long you will be," Collins replied.

I followed Margaret upstairs.

"You really want to rent these rooms?" Margaret asked.

"Are the rooms gruesome?"

"No. But it is over a tavern where men can be rowdy. And sometimes, the Colonel allows some men to stay later than usual. The noise is endless."

"As long as they do not stay past eleven at night, then I will survive."

"Very well, miss. After all, it is *your ears*."

She let me in, and I looked at the two rooms. Going to the window, I looked down to see the prospect down below. I could see far on both sides of the street and could even see the port and ships from there."

I smiled.

"I'll take it."

I looked at Margaret.

"Are you also the chambermaid?"

"Aye," she replied. "I rent next door, so I can come quickly."

"Good. I need another lady who is not far off."

Margaret nodded.

"Understood."

When I went back downstairs, I managed the affairs, Colonel Fitzwilliam told me that he would have papers for me to sign tomorrow when I arrived, and Collins had not left yet. Only this time, he was alone, and his friends must have left. Just as well. I wanted a private word.

I sat down in a nearby chair across from him.

Putting down his mug, Collins looked at me.

"Are you about to lecture me on something?" he asked.

"No," I assured him. "I just want to keep you informed on what I am doing."

Collins raised an eyebrow, amused.

"Really? Well, that is new. You never inform me over anything."

"I do not mean to be hard on you, Will."

"But you are." He sighed. "Any chance you have of forgiving me for what happened at the Massacre? It was years ago, and I did not intend for it to escalate so. I just—"

"Life is complicated," I said. "I am seeing that now. You really want forgiveness, don't you?"

"What man or woman does not want that?"

"Fair point."

I drummed my fingers against the table.

"I understand you a little better now, Will. I just wish things had ended differently."

"But you still do believe in our cause?" he asked, more insistently.

"Always," I assured him.

Collins smiled.

"Well, many do not care what women think, but you know me, Lizzy. I do believe that your voices mean something. My parents did right by me in that way."

"I appreciate that. Truly, I do. And I have to ask you something, as well as tell you something."

Collins leaned forward, interested to know that I was about to take him into my confidence.

"I need confirmation on something," I elaborated. "It's about a mutual friend of ours. A man named Alexander MacDougall."

When hearing the name, Collins flinched.

"What makes you think that I know such a man?" he asked, his voice quiet.

"Because I know you," I whispered. "And you know that

you can trust me. Just nod or shake your head. Are you well acquainted with him?" I asked. "Yes, or no."

Collins's face turned serious. He nodded.

Now it all had been twice confirmed.

"Well," I said, exhausted and resigned, "now I fully know."

Collins leaned over the table and took my hand in his.

"You must understand," he whispered even lower, "Alex loves Charlotte."

His words were heavy, sincere, and was nothing that I did not know already.

"I know," I answered.

"He did not mean to fall in love with her, but he did. You must understand, who could help but fall in love with her?"

"True." Then I began to become amused. "Wait, you are not in love with her too, are you?"

Collins chuckled.

"What? Me? Not in the slightest. I can understand why any other man would fall in love with her, but not this one."

"Really?"

"Yes. It's strange how her beauty does not touch me. But so it is. Oh well, plain women must always have some men to find them attractive. I flatter myself that I am wise for liking women who have to also like me. And plain women like me, so why should I not like them?"

"To love a woman for her virtue rather than through her looks," I considered, "amazing. Even I cannot learn that habit fully. The man must have some comely aspect to him. I can forgive a large belly if he has an amiable and pleasing face. I can forgive a plain face if there is a lot of charm to counteract that."

"Charm!" He snapped his fingers. "Now that I must have. And there has to be something about her character and physique that I have to find: juicy."

"Juicy?" I laughed.

"Yes. A woman must be juicy. I know that makes no sense, but there it is."

He laughed with me.

"Oh," I said, trying to stop my gurgling, "there is another thing."

"What is that?"

"I will remain in Boston for perhaps another month or so. Then I return to Philadelphia."

"So soon?"

"Yes. I cannot stay here. There is too much risk." Suddenly, Captain Darcy's image rose to my mind. The idea of meeting him again filled with me wonder, while also filling me with dread. And I knew what his appearance meant for me: confusion and conflict. "I have this foreboding emotion that something is about to go horribly wrong."

"Understandable," Collins acknowledged, "from our reports, something is about to go horribly wrong."

"What?" I asked, interested and very curious.

"I can tell you nothing now because nothing is certain. But you are right to want to leave in a month. Philadelphia will be a safer place. Have you told Charlotte and Dr. Warren?"

"Not yet. But I am getting to it. I just have to work up the nerve."

"Do it soon. They deserve better."

"True. They do."

I stood up.

"Now it is time for me to leave, or I will be late."

"Late for what?"

"For a man who needs his leg chopped off."

"Oh, so it's that kind of day for you?" he asked.

"Yes, it is that kind of day."

I bid farewell to Colonel Fitzwilliam and thanked him for offering me lodgings.

When I emerged from the Green Dragon, my step was lighter, as well as my mind being heavier.

I had found answers, but I still was to stay here for a month complete. So many things could happen.

Even by not staying at Lucas Lodge, I still was aware that I might see Captain Darcy again, and there would be so much alarm and heated words between us.

Truly, I had never met such an insufferably rude man in uniform. Oh, who was I to say that? For it was clearly not true at all. I had met many a rude character, inclined to being offensive while claiming themselves to be enlightened.

What vexed me was the influence and impact that he had on me. Why was he so often in my thoughts?

Yet it was more than that. His influence seemed to be below my skin, rumbling under the surface and provoking my inner peace at every turn.

Suddenly, I felt goosebumps along my arms despite that I was not cold. The air grew close, and the view of the road felt as if it was growing slender in my vision.

I stopped walking because I knew. I felt him.

Looking to my left, I let my eyes rest on Captain Darcy as he was standing on the other side of the road, sitting atop his horse.

CHAPTER 16

The Question That Is You

Darcy looked upon me.

And I marked him.

Between us was the familiar ache that came from both affecting the other.

Every second felt like an eternity, falling, and rising, like that of a cascade of wonder and starlight that sweeps over nightfall.

However, I did not have an eternity.

I had twenty minutes.

Placing my hands in front of me, and clasping them, I looked *boldly* on him, and spoke *boldly*.

"Well now," I cried, "are you attempting to be obvious? Or was this ill-timed of you?"

He turned his horse around and was about to ride off when I called out to him again.

"There is no point in pretending that you are not curious," I said. "And since I have no choice but to be in the same city as you, we might as well get along. And if the best way to do it is that you cannot bear the sight of me, then so it is. I have done all in my power to lessen our seeing each other, therefore, rejoice. That is all that I have to say."

I walked on.

The best that could be done was not to look at him, but only walk forward, as quickly as could be done. Of course, I had encouraged him by talking to him, and my actions proved to be counterproductive. I spoke in a way that invited Darcy's curiosity. I had but a couple of seconds to realize this, before I heard hoofs approaching me, and soon a beautiful horse had pulled up alongside me and I felt the heat of Darcy's leg as it was near my face.

"What do you mean by that?" he asked me.

"Mean by what, Captain?"

"That you have lessened our company together. You are staying where my officers will be stationed. I gather that you must suffer my company often."

"No, I do not, actually," I replied, lightly and charmingly. "Sir, we shall be free of each other. I have paid for lodgings above the Green Dragon. I shall vacate Lucas Lodge tomorrow and there is no reason to feel as if I taint your company."

"The Green Dragon?" Darcy declared, his voice like a hiss. "No, you cannot do that!"

"I can and I did. No, truly, I really did just do that."

"So that is what took you there?"

"Yes, it is. And I was successful."

"You are a young lady, who ought not to live above a tavern. I will not have it."

"You are not my lord and master!"

"Well, if I was, I would not have let you go. A woman like you needs a husband."

"So that he can lord over me day and night and tell me to come and go when he pleases?" I questioned, angry. "No, I have not resigned myself to that level of servitude." I looked up at him slyly. "Any form of involuntary servitude, especially done at the hands of vicious tendencies to own another, is something that I do *not prefer.*"

My words evidently hit a mark because I saw his face wince.

"You are being saucy," he remarked.

"And you are being unkind, again. You said it yourself; you think that you are better than I. As such, there is no point in conversing with a lady who you find to be beneath you. And I have no desire to be in the presence of a man who does not understand that I am as worthy as him."

"Why do you walk fast?"

"I have to go to work."

"Work? Women work at their homes and yours is in a different colony."

"I work as an assistant. I am a doctor and a surgeon."

"A doctor and surgeon?" he asked, surprised.

"If you are about to say that ladies do not do such things, women are doctors all the time. I am merely a rare one to actually label herself as such."

"You are truly a doctor and surgeon?" he asked.

"I am. And I must not be late to this surgery. A man must have his leg amputated. It's gone gangrene. I work as an assistant to a local doctor."

He stopped his horse.

"Then if you must get there in time," Darcy said, "I offer my services."

He offered me his hand to take.

Stopping, I looked at his hand.

Everything was in that gesture, that brought forth a whirlwind of more sensations that would only cause too much more alarm between us and bewilderment.

Although it brought on something worse. Rejecting him would cause more strife, and I needed to leave here, with roughness turned smooth. However, if I accepted, I would be bringing a redcoat to Dr. Warren's door.

Also, I did despise Darcy.

While also not despising him.

It was enough to make me distraught.

"What is wrong?" he asked. "Who is the person that I am to take you to? Or did you lie to me?"

"You know that I am not lying to you," I replied. "I gather the sense that you are aware that lying to you is not easy."

"No, nor is it easy for me to lie to you. I cannot account for why it would be for your case, but I always believe in telling the absolute truth to all things."

For the first time, I fully looked up at him. His long hair was falling out of his ribbon, and his face did not look angry, but merely curious. His stern scowl had disappeared, and he seemed to genuinely be interested in what I had to say.

"We cannot account for our knowing what is in the other's mind," I noted.

"How do you do that?" he asked.

"What?"

"Always say what is obvious, but no one wants to say."

"I cannot help it," I replied. "It is merely my way. And as for who I am going to, you must understand my apprehension. He is my employer and a good man. But his mere association with me can put him into danger and be scrutinized by redcoats. I do not want him to suffer that."

"Very well. I will merely assume that he is a doctor, and that is all."

Once more, he offered me his hand.

If I did not accept it, I would be late.

Therefore, I took his hand and climbed sidesaddle behind him.

We were off, trotting down the street at a nice but quick pace.

~

"So," I began as we rode. "Were you spying when I saw you, or did I come upon you by mere happenstance?"

"That is the wonder of it," he replied. "I had always considered going to the tavern."

"To spy on your cousin."

"Yes. But that is not why I came today. I could not fathom why, but my instincts compelled me to come today."

"And at this particular time?"

"Yes. I will not even attempt to justify such a rash action. But that is so."

As he rode onward, many British officers walked by, saluting Captain Darcy as he passed them by.

"I will not attempt to justify it either," I replied, ignoring the officers. "You had the feeling that I was there, didn't you?"

Darcy tore his eyes from the road and gave me a sideways glance. Since I was directly behind him, his face was close to mine, and I could feel his breath across my cheek. In fact, his hair whipped across my ear when he turned, and I failed to be insensitive to feeling the proximity of our closeness.

"Yes," Darcy answered, "I did."

Our eyes locked gazes, and I was close to falling into the depths of his, when I recalled myself.

"Pay attention to the road," I answered.

"Very good." He turned back to where we were headed, as I gave him directions. "But that does not change the fact that there is something frightening here. Tell me truly, Miss Bennet, what are you?"

"I told you. I am a Scottish Pennsylvanian."

"Ah, Scottish!" he replied.

"And is this where your prejudice presents itself again?" I questioned.

"Like your people have never been prejudiced towards mine. Scots!"

"English!" I cried, equally as bitter. "Now turn left on this road."

He turned his horse left.

"Miss Bennet, are we about to argue?"

"If you are decided on having one, then so be it. However, we can argue until we are blue, but that will not change anything. Scots have a reason to be angry with the lot of you."

"And we English have a reason to be angry with you. I suppose that it is decided between us that we have been trained to despise the other."

"Perhaps so, but I am not in the mood to suffer under the prejudice of my ancestors," I remarked. "I am still my own woman. Therefore, whatever history that we both come with, I am not going to let that weigh down our conversation. Can we both agree to being equally prejudiced and leave it there?"

Looking at the side of Darcy's face, with my chin rested on his back, I saw a quick flash of contrition pass over his face. Unless I was mistaken, I think that he was happy that I was willing to change the subject and forget the whole encounter.

"I prefer to leave it behind us, so thank you. Forgive me for bringing the issue in between us. I should not have done that. I am sorry."

"Well," I accepted, "as long as you apologize."

Once more, he looked toward me.

"How did you know that my instincts told me that you were at the tavern?"

I was upset that I could not give a logical or sensible answer, but so it was.

"I wish I could satisfy your questions in a way that makes sense in conversation," I answered, "however, I cannot. I just—well, it felt right. It felt like it all made sense, despite not making sense at all."

"I am not unsatisfied. I do understand your meaning. Whether you like it or not, Miss Bennet, but there is something very wrong between us, that I call a connection."

"You call a connection wrong? Oh, that is correct. You find me inferior to you, despite that I am not. No colonist is inferior to anyone from Britain. Those of you who think so are wrong."

"It is just—I am trained to think a certain way."

"You are trained to also think it right to own people. If you believe that is well, then I am not surprised how many of you look on us colonists."

"The Slave trade is what makes Britain, and our American colonies, so wealthy. Why do you scoff at something that brings us so much profit?"

"Profit does not indicate that something is correct. Your mentality is as pernicious as the Indians here."

He looked at me with anger.

"What do you accuse the Indians of? This is *their* land. We are the intruders."

"I was born here, not you. You clearly are not here to see all that they do to us."

"What do they do to us that people like you have not done to them first?"

I was alarmed at this speech. Who was he to talk? He of all people!

"I have done nothing to them."

"But the colonists have. The Indians have no choice but to retaliate for all that we have done."

"It's easy for you to say. You all come here, from overseas, and you judge me, when you have not seen what I have seen. Or lived what I lived. Besides, if the Indians do retaliate for slights that they have felt, who began it? Who do we colonists come from? Who began the conflict?"

Darcy sighed.

"We are about to argue again."

"Yes, evidently we are." For reasons that I could not fathom, I was not in the mood for peace, or for pacifism. I was just angry. And I would not rest until I unleashed my anger, and only then would I have satisfaction.

"You are correct," Darcy acknowledged, "and anything that much of Europe, and our empire, has done can be laid at your feet when it comes to the Indians. We committed wrongs when we landed here—wrongs that scarred the relationships that we ought to have nourished. However, many of us have learned the errors of our ways. But now, the colonists must learn to take some of the responsibility instead of blaming us for everything."

"You began this all."

"And you continue it. You all continue to be at odds with them, never attempting to understand what they have undergone, and experienced. Besides, you call them savage, but how can they be worse than how the Sons of Liberty are? The tar and feathering, the dress up as Indians when throwing the tea off our ships—and led to the crisis that we are experiencing now. The burning of effigies—"

"We inherited that tradition from Britain."

"Even if so, it is improperly done, as well as burning down taxpayers' homes, boycotting British goods, and now look where it has taken Boston? To ruin. How are the Indians worse than that?"

"They have killed too many people that I know," I said simply. "And they killed my mother."

When hearing that, Darcy turned to me, and for the first time, I saw a very different emotion in his face. It was shock, alarm—and concern.

"Oh," was all that he said. "I am sorry."

I sighed heavily as I rested my face against his back, unwilling to look him in the face. Suddenly, I had felt very embarrassed, and I did not want him to see the grief in my eyes.

"Thank you."

"It still hurts to think about, I am sure."

"Of course, it does. Nothing could be more painful."

"Miss Bennet. Might I call you Elizabeth? I am presuming that you might prefer it that way."

"I do. You may call me so."

"Elizabeth, what I am about to say is not meant to hurt you. It is just logic and sense, even though this is not a moment where you want sense. Nothing I say can erase the pain of your mother being taken from you in such a way. That was a terrible thing to happen to you. But not every Indian that you meet is the Indian that killed your mother. It is wrong to blame them all for what the evil of some have done. They are a people, like any other, just with different customs."

"As it is wrong to view the Africans when you purchase them," I retaliated. If he was to humble me, I would not allow him to commit to any sort of hypocrisy. "They did not kill or hurt your people. All offenses caused are you hurting them. Do you not see? I know how it is in Britain. Your plantations are on islands where you cannot see what is occurring, but I have to see it here. And I know it and mark it. The evils, the torture, and all the pain that they undergo is unspeakable. If I am evil for despising the Indians, I do it with my emotions, but your evils are actions. How can you judge me so?"

"And how can you judge me so?"

I groaned.

"No matter what I do, you will continue to think that it is correct to own others, aren't you?"

"No matter what I say, you will continue to think that it is correct to be prejudiced, aren't you?"

"That is not an answer."

"Nor is that an answer."

"Turn on this street and go down it."

He obeyed and rode me near Dr. Warren's house.

"Stop here."

He ordered his stallion to halt.

He read the sign that hung above the windows.

"Dr. Warren's?" He read, dismounting, and turning to me, offering me his hand.

"Yes," I replied, taking his hand as he helped me dismount. "He is my employer. Today, there is to be an amputation. I am helping him."

Darcy did not release my hand as I stepped to the ground.

"I cannot understand how you can be a doctor or surgeon."

"Yes," I replied, "I've heard this before. And I am not in the mood to argue with you again. I am a doctor and surgeon. My father was such, and he trained us to be so, because doctors are always needed. We were not great beauties, so we learned how to make ourselves useful. Besides, I do not think any of us has ever been happy in being too much inside the home. We all feel a little too confined that way."

I looked at our hands, interlocked.

"It's time to let go now," I remarked.

"But," he replied, removing his tricorn hat, "if you are too much around the sick, you can fall ill yourself."

I chuckled.

"And now you are worried about me?"

"I know. I am confusing."

"No," I accepted, "I understand that our interactions will always be strangely provocative and complex. I have come to accept that. Well, we humans rarely ever go a month without falling ill. In fact, I have come to learn that the second we humans are born, we are always dying in one form or another."

"That is morbid."

"I'm a doctor; that is truth. And I could say it while smiling."

I looked to the window, saw Dr. Warren enter the parlor and then he saw me standing there, with Darcy. Both men's gazes met, and I knew that I had to placate the situation immediately —as well as do everything to keep both men from ever meeting.

"Captain," I uttered, "I must tell you that, initially, I did not want you to escort me here."

"Why not? Are you engaged to this man?" His eyes were like slits when he looked down at me.

"No. It is done to protect all those around me. You know my feelings, whether I like that you know them or not. You know where my sympathies lie. Do you know why I am leaving Lucas Lodge? Because I do not want the Lucas family associated with me. Whenever we patriots exist, you assume that everyone connected to us is the same. But that's not so. Dr. Warren is my employer, but he is NOT me. He is not guilty by being associated by me. He ought not to be investigated, nor assumed to be anything else but loyal to Britain."

Everything that I had said was a lie, but I still would not be the ruin of my friend.

"Dr. Warren is my employer and my friend. That is all! He ought not to be in any danger just because he is giving me work. Please, Captain, leave him alone."

Darcy considered.

His next action was entirely unexpected, as he released my hand, walked over to the nearest post, and tied up his horse. Next, he walked up to me and offered me his arm.

"You will understand that I must always inspect things for myself. Also, you claim to be a doctor and surgeon. Well, I wish to see these things for myself. If you have skill, I want to know of it."

I blinked, immediately chagrined at having an audience.

"Really?" I replied. "I cannot help but ask. Why? Why do you prefer to be in the company of a woman that you really do not like?"

One of his hair strands fell from his ribbon and he placed it behind his ear to keep it off his face.

"Maybe I am a glutton for punishment."

"Evidently," I confirmed.

"Like you are any different," he retaliated.

"No," I said, amused. "I am truly not. We really do not like each other, so I am content to keep you out of my life, so that both cause each other less pain."

"Then why do you always smile when I am around?"

"I like smiling. Life would be dull if I didn't. And I despise dullness."

"Do you really hate me?"

I opened my mouth, and then closed it, realizing that I truly did not know what to say to that. Faith, I really did not know. I felt like I hated him, but I genuinely was wholly unaware if I did.

"I hate how you treat me and regard me," I said.

"I can understand that," he said, taking a step toward me. "I have not been very gentlemanlike. Perhaps that is my error. However, do you really hate me?"

I rolled my lip.

"Oh, damn!" I hissed. "I do not hate you."

He smiled.

"I knew it."

I stomped the ground with my foot.

"Fine," I said, "I will ask Dr. Warren if you may stand witness to the amputation procedure. This is his practice, and what he says, goes. However, try not to argue with me again today, and display your sense of superiority—superiority that you have *no right to have*. I cannot suffer too many arguments in one day."

"Elizabeth," he remarked, offering me his arm again, "I cannot agree to that. Our arguments seem to come out of nowhere. How can I prepare for them? Also, I am not in the mood to walk around, having to pay attention to every word that I say. If that be so, I will regret having ever been born."

"You sound like quite the alarmist now," I said, giving in and letting him take my arm and escort me inside.

"You make me so."

"The feeling is mutual."

"True. True."

Darcy opened the door, and we entered Dr. Warren's practice.

This was going to be quite the juggling act for me.

Poor Dr. Warren.

I left, assuring him that I was never going to report his patriotic actions to any British authorities, and now I was walking in —next to a British Captain.

His eyes were glazed over, prepared to be betrayed by someone that he regarded as his friend. I refused to let that impression last.

"Dr. Warren!" I said, smiling, but with anxiety in my eyes. "Would you believe the surprise of it all? I have good news." I removed my cloak and hung it up at the coatrack. "Colonel Fitzwilliam has lent me the rooms."

"Oh."

"And I was met with *another* surprise. After I left the Green Dragon, I somehow managed to come upon the Colonel's cousin, Captain Darcy of the light calvary. He is *also* the main authority to oversee the quartering of the soldiers at Lucas Lodge."

My mouth said all that, but hopefully my eyes were saying, 'Warren, I have been caught in a tight situation, and this is everything that I did not want. Truly, everything that I did not want!'

Fortunately, my eyes said it all.

"Oh, I see."

I introduced both men to each other, pleasantries were exchanged, and the feeling was intense to say the least. All my nerves seemed to tingle between me as a medical patriot and a loyal servant to the crown were in the same room, and each had to tolerate the other.

Once the common phrases were exchanged, I immediately began to explain why a captain in the regulars had escorted me into the building.

"Dr. Warren," I said, "since Captain Darcy felt it incumbent upon himself to escort me here, he also felt a desire to watch our surgery."

My lips were almost a tight line.

"Witness that?" Dr. Warren asked, turning to Darcy. "You wish to sit during our surgery?"

"Yes, I do. According to Elizabeth, you are an accomplished doctor. And her majesty's regiments are in need of doctors in the colonies."

My eyebrows practically shot into my hair.

Darcy was considering Dr. Warren as a doctor to the British soldiers! Now my nerves felt as if they were popping out from under my skin!

"I wish to examine your skill," Darcy furthered. "Also, I have never considered surgery as something that goes unwitnessed. There are many surgeries that tickets are sold to, and people can watch."

"Yes," Dr. Warren said. "That practice. I will never understand us humans and our desire to watch people being cut open and endure such gore. Then again, gladiators at the coliseum were once a long-term practice."

"Humanity has come a long way since then," Darcy countered.

"Yes, but I am not fully certain that we do not regress every once in a while. You wish to observe the surgery?"

"Indeed, I do."

"Very well."

"Where is Mr. Jenkins?" I asked, going into the back room, and returning with an apron and with a handkerchief to cover my mouth with.

"He will be here soon. I have never met an amputee who ever arrives on time. They fear the surgery, so it takes them a long time to come."

"I see your point. They need more time to contemplate their existence of having all their remaining limbs."

"To be sure."

"Very well," I said, going to Darcy and handing him a bucket.

"There's a water pump at the end of the corner. Get some water for your horse. Never fear. The water pump is not too close to a privy pit."

"What does its proximity to a privy pit have to do with water?"

"I do not care what anyone says or what popular habit is. Placing our water wells and pumps near privy pits is what causes our water to be so contaminated. Underground, the waterholes would meet our garbage holes and each other would fuse together."

Darcy considered what I said.

"Actually, that is sound."

I perked up.

"Did you actually agree with me on something?"

"Do not get accustomed to it," he replied lightly. "I do not want you to get disappointed when we argue again."

He left to get water for his horse.

Now that we were alone, I could unveil everything that I was feeling. It all poured forth really quickly, since we did not have much time.

"Well," Dr. Warren said, "we are in a great deal of trouble."

"I am the *one who* is in trouble," I corrected him. "In his eyes, you are just my employer."

"Not in his eyes, perhaps, not. He looks like a hawk. And usually, men like that see like a hawk. He will deduce much while watching us."

"Do your best to remain as innocent looking as you always do, Joseph. And all will be well."

"I am not the only one that I am worried over," he whispered, concerned.

"Thank you, but never fear. I can take care of myself."

"He knows you are a patriot?"

"I had no choice in the matter. He discovered it for himself."

"Then I have a right to worry. How long will it be before he will have *no choice* but to arrest you?"

"You think he will?"

"He will have *no choice*, despite his fascination with you."

"Fascination?" I repeated, astounded. "You think that is what it is? Well, perhaps it is, but not in the traditional manner. He does not hate me, but nor does he like me either. He just does not know how to make me out. I am very different from the ladies he must know in England."

"You are, very much so. But difference can be exotic to some."

"You have just met him. You did not see that all we do is argue and fight."

"That is neither here nor there. You argue, which means that he feels comfortable enough to argue with you. This is not romance that I speak of, but wonder. The way you talk with him makes it evident that he has latched onto you. He will want your company. You have not seen the last of him."

I sighed.

"I know that I have not. How did this happen? I tried so well not to stick out."

Dr. Warren chuckled.

"Elizabeth, you always stick out."

A wagon drove up, and it was Mrs. Jenkins. Mr. Jenkins was in the back and was being helped down by his daughters.

"There is Mr. Jenkins and the women in his family," Dr. Warren said.

"Good," I said, noting the daughters and wife. "We must keep them here. Their presence will help keep Darcy from speaking much to us. We will have weeping ladies on our hands."

"Well, thank the almighty for small favors. This is going to be hard."

"Yes. In more ways than one."

We went out to meet Mr. Jenkins and the ladies just as Darcy approached with the bucket and began to give his horse water.

Now, the surgery would begin, and Darcy would watch. I was being put to the test.

I could not falter now.

CHAPTER 17
Stitched Up

M r. Jenkins proved to be an overweight man, so I did not want to put any strain on his daughters.

"Captain," I announced to Darcy, "can you help Mr. Jenkins in so that I can get the ladies situated?"

"Of course," Captain Darcy replied, patting his horse's neck, then he accosted Mr. Jenkins.

"Good afternoon," Mr. Jenkins said, his head lopping about. Mr. Jenkins accidentally breathed into Darcy's face, and Darcy coughed angrily.

"We had to get him drunk," Mrs. Jenkins explained as I held the door open as Dr. Warren and Darcy helped Jenkins inside. "To dull the pain."

"Yes," Darcy groaned, wanting to hold his nose. "I see."

I tried to suppress my laughter, and Darcy noticed.

"I don't see anything funny about this," he extolled.

"I do."

Despite himself, he could not help but chuckle a little.

Out of the side of my eye, I observed how this did not escape Dr. Warren's notice. Dismissing his powers of observation, I thought it best to get on with the operation and focus solely on that.

"How do you do, Jenkins?" Dr. Warren asked as he and Darcy lumbered Jenkins inside.

"I am fit—fit as a fid-fiddle," Jenkins said, laughing. "I feel —feel as rich as a king today." I opened the door to the surgical room in the back and they brought him inside. "God save the King!" Jenkins cried. Then he looked at Darcy, in his redcoat. "Ah, one of our good soldiers. You do your du—duty, sir?"

"I do, indeed," Darcy replied, as Warren helped Jenkins onto the operating table. I walked over to the knives and axes, and saw that they were in water, but there was no salt in it.

"Good lad, good lad!" Jenkins cried. "You lot will come here and make right all the wrongs on this land. Set all the riffraff straight in this madhouse. Set this place right, sir. Set this place right."

Despite that the man was drunk, Darcy naturally could not help but feel a sense of elation in hearing such approval.

Naturally, his chest swelled, and he gave me a proud look.

"We shall, and I thank you for having proper pride in loyalty to the empire."

I returned Darcy's look with a saucy one of my own.

"Tsk, tsk, tsk," I muttered as I left, rushed to the kitchen, and got some salt.

Returning to the room, I poured salt over the blades and placed them into the water as Dr. Warren was strapping Jenkins onto the table.

"Lizzy?" Warren asked.

"It was a practice that my father employed," I explained, "salt on a wound is agony, but salt water purifies. It cleans medical utensils and prevents infection."

"He thought so?"

"Yes," I said, "please do not be angry with me for believing him, but I think he was correct. None of the men he amputated ever grew infection or developed sepsis. Can—can we try it today?"

Warren bit his lip.

"Well, if salt keeps meat from going bad, then the late Mr. Bennet was probably onto something. Let us try it."

Unable to resist, I stole a look at Darcy, and saw that he was watching me most acutely. No doubt he heard of what I said.

It would only be natural for me to be intimidated by the Jenkins women. After all, this was their husband and father that I was going to assist in cutting a limb off. But it was not so. I was terrified of Darcy being there. Suddenly, I grew nervous and was happy that I did not have to do the cutting. Yet, I had to do everything else, and it still required a steady hand.

Once we gave Jenkins as much tonic as we could to numb the pain, there would still be a great deal of shouting. I rolled up a rag and placed it in his mouth so that he could bite down on it and not chip his teeth, nor bite his own tongue.

Turning to the Jenkins women, Dr. Warren asked them if they really wished to be present for this. Mrs. Jenkins ordered her daughters to leave, but she would remain, for she had seen such horrors before.

The daughters left, I placed the Petit Tourniquet above the infected leg (Jean Louis Petit, thank you so much for inventing that tourniquet), made sure that there was a hot Sad Iron in the fireplace for me to cauterize the wound, and all was ready.

Dipping my hands in the salt water to clean them, (to which Dr. Warren repeated that), I handed him the clean scalpel, and I placed my hands in a circular motion around Jenkins's leg, so that Warren knew where to cut.

Warren placed the blade just above where my hands were, around the entire leg.

I looked at Captain Darcy.

"Still willing to watch?" I asked.

"I'm a captain; you're not doing anything that I have not seen many times over."

"Very well. Play the 'strong man'."

"I am a strong man."

"Let me be the judge of that."

Turning back to Warren, I was prepared. We pulled back the skin that he had cut, like that of a stocking. Underneath, the blood and muscle were revealed.

Mrs. Jenkins made a repulsive sound, covering her mouth.

"Mrs. Jenkins," I said, "if you are about to purge up your food—"

"No," she assured me, "sorry, this is just the first reaction. Besides, soon, you will need me to help hold him down. It will not be long now, will it?"

"Never fear, Dr. Warren is quick when it comes to cutting."

Once we had fully peeled back all the skin, I rushed to the salt water, removed the axe, and quickly handed it to Dr. Warren.

"Mrs. Jenkins," I said, "hold down your husband's right arm, and hold down his other leg."

"Indeed," Mrs. Jenkins said, breathing in heavily. She did as I ordered, and then I began to pry open all the muscle so that Warren could get to the bone.

Jenkins's screams were long.

Once I pulled back enough muscle and tissue, the bone was revealed. Dr. Warren placed the surgical axe on the leg and quickly began to saw the man's calf off.

No matter how drunk a man is, that's a pain that no beer can overpower. Jenkins began to flail as Warren tried to remove the limb.

Doing the best that I could, I still held down his leg so that Warren could get the best cut.

After forty seconds, Dr. Warren got the limb removed, cast it onto the floor over a large bit of canvas, I rushed to the fireplace, got the Sad Iron, dashed back to the operating table, and pressed it against the wound.

Jenkins cried out. Thank God for that rag stifling his cries even more! If it weren't for that, everyone on the street would think that we were torturing someone.

Once I knew that the wound was closed, I removed the press, but I knew that Jenkins would still be flailing around.

"Captain," I ordered Darcy, "I need you to hold Jenkins down as we roll down his skin."

"Of course," Darcy said, removing his redcoat quickly, and taking my place.

Now that my arms were secure, I assisted Dr. Warren as we rolled down the skin we had pulled back, closed it over the stump, and then I began to close the wound with an adhesive.

Within an hour's time, the amputation had fully ended.

It's a truth, known by all medical practitioners, that a patient cannot just get up and walk away after an amputation. They need at least an hour in the chair to collect their strength. As well as being given something to eat and drink to get their energy back.

Above all, they need to be left alone, because they are in so much pain, they cry.

Mr. Jenkins was a big man. Showing weakness was unlike him. Therefore, when he began to weep into his wife's arm, Dr.

Warren turned away from him and went to get his daughters, while I went to the kitchen to gather some dried meats and cheese to eat. And of course, some more beer.

"That was quick," Darcy said as he followed me into the kitchen.

"A surgeon is as much admired for his speed as he is for his skill," I said, going into the larder and getting some meat and cheese. "And always give an amputee meat or cheese after the surgery. They need the nourishment."

"I can see why."

He followed me back to the room and we entered quickly. I gave the food to one of the daughters, picked up the utensils, placed them back in the saltwater, then took it back to the kitchen.

"Follow me again," I ordered Darcy.

"You have no right to order me about," Darcy said, *following* me.

"You did as I requested."

"I know, but still. I am the officer here."

"And I am the doctor. When a surgery has ended, I still have the authority. And that man is not your officer. And nor am I."

I began to clean the axe, knives, and other items in the wash basin.

"No, you are not," he said, laughing. "A lady fighting as an officer."

"Tell that to Joan of Arc. And Penthesilea as well as the other amazons."

"We are not the Ancient Greeks or the French."

"Was it not you who said that difference does not mean wrong?"

I flicked some water at him.

"Hey!" he bellowed, flicking some water at me. I was not one to lose. So, I splashed more water at him.

He returned the gesture.

It reached such a pitch that we were on the verge of laughing hysterically.

"I just realized that we are hurling water at each other that has blood in it," I acknowledged.

"Yes, we really must stop."

"We ought to, and we will."

I began to dry the utensils.

"You did well," he said.

"Is that another compliment?"

"Come now, Elizabeth. There is no need to sound so terribly rough. Can you not say thank you?"

I sighed.

"Now, who is the one to do the ordering?"

"That's correct," he allowed, "I am not your master. Your lord and master."

"Thank you," I said, after the fact. "For the compliment."

He walked up to me and leaned against the wall, facing me. "You're welcome."

I did not smile, but I looked softly on him before I continued drying.

"How did it make you feel?" he asked.

"The surgery? Well, I confess that your being there made me nervous, but once I began, my nerves faded. Now, if it was me who had to do the cutting this time, then maybe I would have been more apprehensive."

"You've amputated before?"

"Yes. Back home in Philadelphia. I had to amputate an arm and a leg once. It took four men to hold the second patient down, even with the straps. He was that strong."

"A real Heracles."

"A real Heracles."

"No, actually, when I asked how it made you feel, what I

had referred to was when Jenkins praised me for coming here to keep the peace and suppress the rebellion?"

"It is nothing that I have not heard of before. And even from friends of mine here and in Philadelphia."

"You have?"

"Yes. Many of the colonists are very loyal to the king. Including the Lucas family and there is a family in Philadelphia, the Drinkers. They are Quakers. They are not on either side, fully, but they do believe in keeping the peace, at all costs."

"Ah, Quakers!"

"I gather you do not respect them."

"I admire their attempts for being peacekeepers, but there is a reason that we were happy when they left England in droves. They refused to go into the service or bow to any superior."

"There are Quakers in London."

"Yes, but not as common as they once were."

"My father was a Quaker," I said. "He was what was called a Public Friend. My mother converted when they married and became a Public Friend as well. Public Friends can be both male and female. They are the Quakers that can move about the ministry, preaching to and attempting to convert and reform the larger society that they are in."

"Oh," Darcy said, "I meant no offense. We are about to argue again, aren't we? After all, then you must be a Quaker as well."

"I was, before I was kicked out."

"What?"

"I was born a Quaker and raised as one. But I was thrown out. I would prefer that you do not take a prejudice towards them. They have every right to be here, and respected, but you are not going to engage in a holy war with me. I cannot argue something that I am no longer a part of."

I began to put away the utensils when Darcy leaned closer to me.

"Might I ask why?" he asked. "Why were you thrown out?"

"There were practices that I did not agree with."

"Such as?"

"Well, I never understood the inclination of why we could not practice Christmas."

"You all don't?"

"We are trained to believe that no day is holier than the other. So, we ought not to celebrate Christmas. But I cannot help but find Christmas to be a delightful diversion. It's more to me like a day of being able to celebrate what we've arrived at. It is almost as if the day is more than just Christ's day. It's also a day of showing that we made it to the end of the year, and that we are still prosperous and can enjoy each other's company over food and good cheer. But my lectures did not go over well. As well as that I believed that we ought to have the right to have musical instruments in our home."

"Quakers do not believe in having instruments in the house?"

"We practice simplicity."

"There is nothing wrong with music."

"I know," I allowed. "I cannot fathom why. But that was not enough to have me kicked out of the faith. The last thing was a true grievance in their eyes."

"And what was that?"

"I did not believe that the Quaker Meeting had any right to dictate who we marry."

∾

When hearing this, Darcy's eyes grew more alert.

"What?" he asked, agog.

"Yes. According to Quaker tradition, if we Quakers wish to marry, not only do we need approval of both parents or guardians, but we also must get the approval of the Quaker Meeting."

"And by the Quaker Meeting, you refer to all the other Quakers in your congregation."

"Yes. All the other friends in the meeting. The couple who wish to marry is required to appear before two monthly meetings before the marriage is approved. It's called 'passing the meeting'."

"And you disagreed with that?"

"Yes. I did. I did not disagree with the idea of going to the two monthly meetings, but I did disagree with needing the whole group of Friends approving who someone wishes to marry."

"I can well understand why. What if someone in the meeting has taken a natural dislike to the person the other chooses to marry?"

"Precisely!" I agreed. "We all speak about equality, but there are still flaws. Human flaws. And human disagreements. I understand your parents having a say, but that is all. And even then, I would still say that it ought to be left solely to the couple."

"And when you marry, you thought they would have no right to order your life?"

"Me and others."

"Were you planning to choose a man at this time for a husband?"

"I had no prospects, nor was I looking for any prospects. I argued out of mere general concern. It led to me being written out of the Meeting."

Darcy squinted at this revelation.

"You were hurled out because you were outspoken, by a

faith that began in Britain by people who were always being so outspoken. Well, that is another bit of irony that you have laid on."

"My colony was founded on irony," I continued, "so I ought not to be surprised."

"Pennsylvania?"

"Aye." Suddenly, I realized something, and I slapped my forehead. "Oh, that reminds me! I almost forgot."

"What?"

"A letter. I have received letters from Philadelphia, and I forgot to read one of them. It's from a friend of mine."

"Who would the friend be?"

"Betsy Ross."

Rushing to my market wallet, I began to search frantically.

"Hopefully, I did not lose it."

Feeling around, I pulled out my letters and saw Betsy's name on one of them.

Chuckling, I put it back.

"Good. I have not lost it."

"What about our conversation reminded you about her letter?" Darcy asked me.

"Like me, she was also kicked out of the meeting."

"This Betsy Ross was also a Quaker who was kicked out of your faith? What did she do? Play on the pianoforte?"

"No, she did an extreme version of what I preached. She eloped and married a non-Quaker."

"Eloped?"

"Yes. Her husband, John Ross, was an Anglican. He attends Christ Church of England, in Philadelphia. They were both apprentices in an upholstery shop, they fell madly in love, and were forbidden from marrying, because he was an Anglican. We Friends also believe that we cannot marry others of a different faith. This led to Betsy and John eloping, running to New Jersey, and marrying in Hugg's Tavern."

"She married her husband in a tavern?!"

"Yes. She went in as Betsy Griscombe and walked out as Betsy Ross. This was November, last year, and she was kicked out of the meeting by the end of that month. I was kicked out a few months prior. In March of 1773."

"My word!"

"Yes. Two women named Elizabeth, who went to the same meetings, were kicked out in the same year. Except that I go by Lizzy and Eliza, and she goes by Betsy."

When hearing this, Darcy did something I never would have foreseen. He burst out laughing.

∾

At first, I scoffed, indignant.

"This is not comical, sir!"

"I am heartily sorry, but yes, it is," he continued, laughing. "Two Elizabeths kicked out of the same Quaker Meeting in one year. That is priceless!"

"No, it's… no it's…" I began to laugh as well. "Oh, very well, it is. Isn't it?"

"Yes. I am sorry for your pain, but it cannot be helped. And you mock me for being tyrannical."

"Parliament and the King are tyrannical."

"Yes, but you have even managed to be expelled by your own people. Is that not the epitome of irony?"

"I regret nothing, except that it disappointed my father. But even he understood."

"Your father sounds like a good man."

"He was." I stopped laughing, remembering him. "My father was a good man. A true Quaker. And not a false abolitionist, but a real one."

"What do you mean?" he asked, growing serious from hearing me say the word 'abolitionist'.

"Well, even those who preach about equality still view the negroes as being inferior to us. My father was no hypocrite. He did not believe that. Again, as you say, they are just different."

When hearing our tone turn serious, Darcy quieted down.

"The merriment has quite gone out of the conversation now."

"You are angry with me for that, aren't you?" I asked.

"Well, yes, if you must know. We were getting along."

"I know."

"But you cannot judge me too much. You come from Quakers, and they are practically puritans."

Instantly, I grew on the defensive to stand by a faith that I was cast out of.

"No, I cannot allow that. Friends are not puritans. The faith is sound; it is humans that bring the flaws to it. Like any faith, I believe Quakerism is no different."

"I suppose, well, you must understand that I have never met a Quaker so closely. I must admit that I do not entirely know what the faith entails, other than what you have told me. Which I am utterly against."

"It's not your fault. Many people do not explain us well. Quakers gather to experience the inner light. It is a spiritual state, and it is a Christian-based religion. We do not trust set prayers, or an ordained ministry, because we do not need one. Since we believe that the light is within all man and woman, there is no need for a priest to lead the service. Because no one is higher than another. We believe in peace, not war. At our meetings, we all gather. The tradition is that we sit in silence, letting the heavenly beliefs fill us, but this is rare. There is always someone who stands up and speaks about anything that they care deeply about. There are Quaker ministers, who feel it their divine right to speak, but we all pretty much do that. The Quakers wrote me out of their meeting, but I can still walk about in society and Quakers still speak to me. Unlike the puritans, who if you argue against them, they will destroy you. And for a certain time, they would have branded you a witch and burned you at the stake. At least I just got written out."

"Ah, yes. Salem!"

"Yes," I replied, bitter. "Salem! Say what you will about Pennsylvania, but we only had one witch trial, and she was acquitted."

"She was?"

"Yes. Her name was Margaret Madsen. She was an older Swedish lady. And between her not knowing much English, and her mental faculties leaving her at a late age, she was known for being regarded as strange. And one person even claimed to have seen her hopping around on a broomstick once. Eventually she was accused of being a witch. She was put on trial, the accusers were all very idiotic, and she was declared guilty of having the fame of being a witch, but that she was innocent of actual witchcraft. Simply put, she was only guilty of being known as a witch, but she was not a witch at all. She was declared innocent, and that was the first and last witch trial that Pennsylvania had."

"Well, that is an amusing story."

"Yes. And even more amusing is that the judge of the trial was Governor William Penn, who was the English Quaker who founded Pennsylvania."

"He presided over it?"

"Yes, he did. He trusted in trial by jury, and it worked out in his favor, because he did not want the hunt in his own colony.

And thus, Pennsylvania colony escaped the horror of the witch trials."

"I like that story."

"I thought you would," I replied, smiling fondly at him.

"Ahem!"

We turned to who was clearing his throat and it was Dr. Warren standing in the doorway. How long he had been there, we did not know.

"Jenkins is now ready to leave. We should escort his family outside."

"Understood," I said, taking out an apple from the storage. I tossed it to Darcy. "For your horse."

Darcy pocketed the apple, and we followed Dr. Warren out.

When we escorted Jenkins and his family to the wagon, Darcy turned to Dr. Warren as he fed his horse.

"Is Miss Bennet's services still required, or can I escort her back to Lucas Lodge?"

Dr. Warren gave him a significant look.

"I have no more appointments today. Lizzy, you must come tomorrow after settling in at the Green Dragon. I need us to mix some medicine and tend to a few patients that I have in the afternoon."

"Shall I come by eleven?"

"That would be perfect." Dr. Warren turned to Darcy. "Captain, I leave my assistant in your charge. Keep her safe."

"That will be easy for me," Darcy answered curtly.

He got on his horse and offered me his hand.

Well, there was nothing for it.

Clasping my cloak under my neck, I made my farewells kindly to Warren, took Captain Darcy's hand and mounted behind him.

"I hate that we have to ride sidesaddle," I said.

"I had a feeling that you would."

We rode off, down the street.

"By the way," I said, "I have to ask something that I always wanted to ask."

"What?"

"Is your first name really Fitzwilliam?"

Darcy did not respond.

"Well," I pressed, "is it?"

"Yes."

"Oh, you poor boy."

"I know," he grunted. "Why did my parents have to do that, I shall never understand."

"And to think, for the longest time, I regretted being named Elizabeth."

"Why?" he asked, surprised.

"There are many Elizabeths in the world. I always was jealous of girls whose names were not the same name as every girl in the yard. But now, I count my blessings."

"Yes, you really ought to. I try to avoid letting anyone know my first name. The things that people say about me, behind my back, is too trying for me."

We rode on.

CHAPTER 18
Leaving the Lodge

When Darcy and I arrived at Lucas Lodge, we were met by Sergeant Bingley exiting the house.

"Captain?" Bingley asked.

"Sergeant Bingley. Has all been well since I've been gone?"

"Yes. All arrangements have been made. And you bring a lady behind you."

"A doctor as well, apparently."

"Doctor?" Bingley repeated, as Darcy dismounted and helped me down. This time, he took me by the waist, without even giving me the chance to argue.

"Yes, you heard correctly," I said, walking up to Bingley. Instinctively, he was on his guard. I knew what he was about.

I shifted to the right.

He jumped in the same direction.

I jumped to the left.

He shifted in my path.

We repeated this until I shifted in one direction, then jumped in the other and I rushed past him, to the door.

"Victory!" I cried, raising my fist up, triumphantly.

"I let you win," Bingley responded.

"You may tell yourself that," I said, opening the door, "if that gives you comfort."

"What was that about?" Darcy asked.

"It's a game we play, Captain," Bingley said, still smiling at me. "Miss Bennet likes me, I believe."

"No, she does not!" Darcy snapped. It led to Bingley and I looking at him, startled. This led to Bingley straightening up and trying to appear more professional.

"Forgive me if I was being uncouth, sir," he rushed out.

"I shall go in," I said, trying to untangle myself from any awkwardness. "I think the moment has reached a strange pitch."

As I walked in, I overheard Bingley approach Darcy.

"Forgive me, Bingley," Darcy said. "I cannot explain why I spoke so censoriously before."

"Thank you, Captain. If I may ask, is something wrong?"

I did not take the time to listen in, because I knew that what ought to be done could not be done too quickly.

Closing the door behind me, I was immediately set upon by Charlotte, who came rushing down the stairs.

"Lizzy," Charlotte said, "I saw you coming from the window and on Captain Darcy's horse. I do hope you both have arrived at some sort of understanding."

"What you and I call understanding means two very different things," I said. "We did arrive at something, but I am not certain what it is. All I know is that we have not grown to be afraid of each other. And that is a start. Charlotte, you must gather all the family. I have an announcement to make."

"You and your announcements," Charlotte pointed out, smirking. "How do you manage it?"

"By going outside whenever I get the chance."

"Well," Charlotte said, merrily taking my arm, "we also have a visitor."

"Charlotte, did you find your shawl?" A voice said from the parlor. A familiar voice.

Going to the parlor, I saw Alex MacDougall sitting by the pianoforte and tapping the keys.

Uh oh.

"Lizzy?" Alex said, standing up, "I did not know you arrived."

"I did. I was escorted by Captain Darcy, of the British light calvary."

A quick disquiet flashed across his eyes before it was replaced by false indifference.

"Oh. More British officers shall be living here? That is a lot for the Lucas family to take on."

"Apologies, Alex," Charlotte said, poking her face in the doorway. "I forgot to bring my shawl downstairs. I shall bring it down soon."

Again, she rushed back upstairs.

"I asked her to show me a shawl that she purchased," Alex explained. "It arrived from India."

"It is lovely. Like her wedding gown."

"I cannot wait to see it," Alex said, clapping his hands together. "And I—"

I rushed to him, taking his arm to silence him as I grew serious.

"Lex," I stressed, "you have to tell Charlotte the truth. I know what you are. We both are the same in that way. But Charlotte deserves to know."

When hearing my pleas, Alex's eyes turned serious.

"I know," he whispered. "But... how can I, Lizzy? I will lose her."

"I know that is a possibility. Perhaps she may still love you, despite it all."

"How can she? She's a loyalist. She is trained to despise what I stand for. And even if she still might love me, her parents will be against it. I love her. If I wait until we marry—"

"That is not fair to trap her. And you know it. If you tell her after the fact, then she will not be given the choice."

He sighed.

"By God, why does this have to be so complicated?"

"I know this is hard," I empathized. "But you have to do this."

He rubbed his face, frustrated.

"Damn it all," he swore. "You know what's horrible?"

"What?"

"That you are right. Well, give me a couple days, Lizzy. Please, give me that time."

"I will. But if you do not, I will have no choice, Lex. I will have to tell her myself."

We were interrupted when hearing Charlotte come down the steps.

We separated and Charlotte brought in the shawl, which Alexander complimented sincerely.

I moved away from them, to give them time alone, as I sat down and began to read my last unread letter:

Dear Lizzy,

Well, it is more of the same with me, as well as a little of the new.

If you have already heard this, then forgive me for repeating this.

The governor in Massachusetts, Thomas Hutchinson, is now as famous in Philadelphia as he must be in Boston. News has spread of his failure to oppose British taxation policies. It has created a lot of hostility in a few port cities, and our city is no different than any other.

On May 2nd, here in Philadelphia, a wooden effigy of Hutchinson was made, with a plaque raised over the large doll, describing him as a traitor to his native country. It was carted around the town, paraded through the streets, and burned in the middle of a large crowd.

While I do agree that taxation without representation is awful, I do not agree with the burning of effigies. As I know that you do not.

I think quite a few of us Pennsylvanians sympathize with the Bostonians, but I cannot speak of other colonies. For who could? We each of us are like our own country.

Onto other matters, my family never stopped talking to me, which is fortunate. I daresay that my parents have forgiven me for marrying John. Some Quakers are still kind toward me and refuse to cast me out.

As to some other Quakers in our city, I find that their resentment is almost akin to being implacable.

You would think that I would come upon that familiar thing like regret. But I cannot humor them and am happy not to. John is the love of my life. Even when we argue, he is such.

And that brings me to another matter to discuss, which is our history. It is a matter of contrition on my part, that it took me some time to accept and confront you about. You know how it is with us humans. There are some things that ought to be said, but we are too ashamed to say it. Therefore, that is was letters are for! It is easier to write them.

Lizzy, when you were cast out of our Friendly Meeting, I was like everyone else, was I not? I did not hate you, to be sure, but I was a little cold to you, not understanding why you were so adamant.

Especially since you had done nothing nearly as scandalous as my sister had done when she also gave into her spirited nature and married her husband at a Baptist church. But on that point, it is best to be silent. Deborah has moved on and we accepted her. This already makes my coolness towards yourself even more double in standard.

And then I fell in love with John, to the point where I could not resist marrying him. And then everything else happened, and I suffered the same fate that you have.

And you were the first to be there for me, at such a difficult time. You sympathized, you understood. And we fell into the way of being alike in more ways than name.

You were better than I, in those moments. You were there for me when I was not as warm to you. For that, I ask for forgiveness. I have been humbled and have given into my spirited nature and willingness to follow what I believe is correct for me, which is different than the path that I once sought. I am sorry for not being as clearsighted as you were, for a time. But I am here now, and I ask that you know that I am better. I am more forgiving of the whims of human nature and not as distant.

I have my principles, and morals, to be sure. But I am more accepting, now that I have been dismissed by our fellow people. I see the need for a little resistance to the oppressive, to rise against the extreme, and the willingness to question— but also to still be kind.

I am better now than I had been, and I will not turn my back upon you so again. Forgive me for being foolish before.

Remember me as I am, rather than how I have been.

Your friend,

B. Ross

Ps – Alice is still alive in case you have not been told. She is still as strong as ever and still steers the ferry. Also, there is a new arrival in my life. I have recently made the acquaintance of one Esther Reed. She is from London, but she sympathizes with our American quests for equality or representation. I shall speak more with her as time goes by. I think we have an ally in her.

~

Closing the letter, I set it down in my lap, contemplating what Betsy had written.

After all those months, she finally wrote what I knew that she was feeling for quite some time.

We heard footsteps and quieted down when Captain Darcy entered.

"Forgive the intrusion."

Alex gave me a sharp look and masked it with amiable tones.

"Of course. You are among the officers who is to stay here at the Lodge?"

"No, I remain at General Gage's headquarters. My officers will remain here."

"Though I am not this house's lord and master, I welcome you and hope that you have enjoyed Boston."

"Thank you, but I have not had time for gaiety. The rebels have kept us quite on our toes, but soon, all shall be rectified."

Alex swallowed, but it was a small gesture, which only I knew what it signified. He was swallowing his anger.

"Very good, sir. I pray that you are successful."

"Thank you."

Turning away from the couple, Captain Darcy approached me and offered me his arm.

"Miss Bennet, might I persuade you to take a turn about the room?"

"Walk around the room?" I asked, to clarify. "That is what you refer to, correct?"

"Yes. It is quite refreshing."

He offered me his arm, and I took it instinctively.

"You have a difficult problem, don't you?" I asked, walking about the room with him.

"What is that?"

"You have grown accustomed to my company, haven't you?"

"Yes, I daresay that I have."

"I am so sorry for you. This must be very inconvenient."

"I do not attempt to deny that. You have made my life a little complicated, but I have gathered a strong understanding and will not fall prey to follies. At the end of the day, I will do my duty."

"I know that you will. It is best to commit to one's cause."

"Are we really on two different sides?"

"I think we might be. Will you have me arrested for it?"

"I am not in the habit of arresting women because of their beliefs."

I looked at him, and I daresay that I admired that speech.

"Thank you," I said, warmly. "I appreciate that gesture. It is not treason to want equality on all counts."

"I still cannot agree with you."

"That I know and accept. As long as you do not try to convince me either, then that is all that I ask."

"Well, I am not certain of that."

"You are not?"

Darcy swiped the air.

"But no more of that. Let us talk of other things. When I

entered, you were lowering your letter. Did you have the chance to read it?"

"I did."

"And it is from your friend, the seamstress?"

"Upholsterer," I clarified. "Betsy is an upholsterer. But it is an easy mistake to make. To be sure. She is quite skilled actually. She also wrote to tell me that a mutual acquaintance of ours still lives. She is a slave in Pennsylvania, and her name is Alice. Her master never fully wrote down her birthday, but by all that she remembers, she must be at the very least 88 years old."

"And she is healthy?"

"As a horse, and that is the wonder of it. She even still works. She's called Alice of Dunk's Ferry, because she is the ferry driver who controls the ferry to take people from Pennsylvania to New Jersey. Everyone knows her and historians go to her because she is the only one who was alive when Pennsylvania was just becoming a colony. She even met William Penn."

"The founder of Pennsylvania?"

"Yes. The same man who presided at Margaret Madsen's trial. Alice was working at the ferry when she met him. People ask her what he was like. She said that he was respectful but could easily rouse to being emotional. It was not a slight on her part, but just descriptive. She said that she spent the whole time talking to him and was happy when she made him laugh. Apparently, he liked to laugh."

"So that is the Londoner who found your colony."

"She only met him for an hour. Alice mentioned what she knew and only what she knew. Either way, she is the only one who saw Philadelphia as it was just becoming a city. Imagine, to grow up and see the whole world change."

"We are seeing the world change as we speak."

"True," I admitted, still looking at the letter, "it is."

"If I am not being too bold, might I ask what else is on your mind?"

Since what I was about to say was heavy, I sat down. He joined me, by sitting in a chair next to mine.

"It has to do with something else that Betsy mentioned. I feel so exposed now."

"Exposed?"

"Do you ever wonder what it is like when someone apologizes, and you cannot help but feel a little apprehensive. You appreciate it, and you even want to hear it, but now that you do, you do not know how to react, for fear of being uncomfortable."

"I think that I do. Nothing is harder than apologizing or being the one who has to be on the receiving end as well."

"Well, when I was first written out of the Quaker meeting, Betsy and I were not on friendly terms. She never cast aspersions at me or criticized me. But she was a little cool toward me. It was more so that she was distant, or never seeking me out. She smiled at me and nodded, but I knew that she was confused on how to approach me. I felt like she wanted to speak to me but did not know how to go about it. Then she eloped, and when she returned, equally as dismissed, I made it a point to show her solidarity. I was there for her. And now she apologizes because she had not always been there for me. However, she apologized and now she understands."

"What?"

"Me. She understands me."

"I take it that you are happy over it, but also apprehensive."

"I did appreciate it, but how do I act when I see her again?"

"As you always do," Darcy assured me, "through your own instinct."

Lowering the letter, I stared boldly at him. So much so, that

I think I startled him, which made him feel uncomfortable. I was not surprised.

"Why do you stare at me so?" he asked. "Are you studying my face?"

"I am making you uncomfortable."

"Yes. I cannot help but confess this."

"Good."

He raised an eyebrow.

"Good?"

"I am staring at you. You had better be nervous. You would not be a gentleman if otherwise."

He blinked, leaning a little forward.

"What is the meaning of this? Are you trying to toy with me?"

"Of course, I am," I answered without any sense of surprise. If anything, I dare say that I must have sounded charming, by accident. "I always am. It's my skill and I am going to wear it proudly. You see, that's the drawback to when you tell someone that you regard yourself as being superior to them. A lesser person will agree with you, but I am not in the mood to be so blindly yielding. You claimed to be superior, and believe it or not, you have lost power over me. In its place is defiance. But I was not made for ill humor, even when you put me in it. Therefore, I do believe that my tone will always be to tease you, by way of torment." I rolled my head a little. "You really brought this on yourself, you know."

At his wit's end, Darcy stood up—and I do believe that was the quickest I had ever seen him move!

He paced to the window, back and forth twice before he turned back to me.

"I cannot win here, can I?" he groaned.

"No," I said, stifling back laughter, "you cannot."

Judging from his expression, he was rolling his tongue behind his teeth.

"You take delight in this, do you not?"

"Indeed, I do."

Suddenly, his face turned serious, and he walked up to me and clasped his hands behind his back.

"Elizabeth, I am sorry."

My chuckles fell inside of my throat and were swallowed.

"Sorry for what?"

"For calling you unequal. I see that I was making a generalization on you colonists as a whole rather than seeing you all as individuals. When we are all equal subjects of the British Empire. I never should have regarded you as unequal to myself, and I ask for your forgiveness."

When hearing him say that, I felt as if my skin had turned as white as snow.

He was apologizing. And it had taken me quite by surprise.

"You mean that?" I asked, astounded.

"Aye, I do."

"Well, I had better accept it. I really ought to—oh, I am saying all the wrong things. If only the King and Parliament had considered us so, there would be no conflict, and..."

"You are letting all come out now," he asked, sitting down, "apologies are still hard for you?"

Suddenly, his eyes darted to Betsy Ross's letter, and I saw. I saw!

Roused to being almost duped, I pinched his knee, which shocked him to no end.

"You do not touch a gentleman," he gasped.

"Stop pretending to be offended," I retaliated. "I saw! You

had a strategy. I told you about feeling awkward in hearing Betsy's apology, and how disconcerted I was. And then you apologize a moment later." I pursed my lips. "Strategy to disorientate me."

His eyes shifted from false offense, to the look of a trickster.

"Perhaps," he said, a hint of innocent malice in his voice.

"You asp!" I hissed. "You are like Henry the Second, aren't you?"

"You know of him?"

"Oh, I very much know of him! Who would not know of the man who married Queen Eleanor of Aquitaine? Now *that* was a *woman*."

"I should have known that you would admire such a woman. A woman who led civil wars against her own husband."

"He deserved it."

"Would you commit civil wars on me?"

I rubbed my face.

"First, I fear that you would be the one to begin the first offense. Second, you are distracting me. You knew that an apology, delivered in such a way, would disorientate me. And you wanted to see me that way."

"Perhaps I did. It amused me."

"Well, I do not deny that it was well-played." I was still annoyed with him, but again, I was still amused through it all. "But if you meant it, then I appreciate it. I do so wish that many more from the Empire shared such a sentiment."

"Please, let us not talk of unpleasant things now," he said. "We have been getting along."

"Never fear," I said, "even when we argue—which I know that we will do again, I want you to know that I am not your enemy. I will not hurt you."

"You talk about me like I am weak. I flatter myself that I am a strong man who would not be so easily hurt by a lady."

"I have found that we women can hurt you as hard as men. The world assumes that we are weak, so we allow you to think of such. But in the end, we can be just as forceful and vicious as you men can be. In fact, I am convinced that the only thing that throws us to the parlor and confines us there is that you men are born stronger, and we are the ones who bear the children. If it were the reverse, then we would dominate you lot and you would shout out oppression."

"Stop being strange!" he said sharply, but it was obvious he was hiding that he was amused and found me diverting.

"Well, I am strange," I pursued, determined to make him squirm in his seat. How I took delight in vexing him! Being evil sometimes can be a delight. "I am the strangest creature in the world. Perverse and not worthy of your company. You ought to leave me. You ought to walk away and never come into my life again. I am angry that horses are not purple. I do not understand why God invented mosquitoes and that they should all be destroyed. Truly, they serve no earthly purpose but to destroy everything. I wish that every household had four cats in it. Then I wish that mistletoe only worked if it was hung from a milliner's shop. And that you, Captain Darcy, were born in the Colonies and ran around the countryside shouting 'I am fortune's fool'!"

"I hate Romeo," he said unable to stop laughing, since I had quoted Romeo from *Romeo and Juliet*.

"Who does like Romeo?" I replied, laughing as well.

"What goes on over there?" Charlotte asked from the other side of the room, still holding hands with Alexander.

"Truly, we must have our share in the conversation if it is amusing," Alexander declared.

"Oh, it's nothing worth repeating," I determined. "I was just making a statue laugh."

"I am not a statue," Darcy declared.

"Have you looked in the mirror lately?" I returned.

"You are a witch," he declared.

"This is Massachusetts; don't hang me."

"I am British; I just might."

Charlotte's eyes lit up in seeing me get along with Captain Darcy. While it also made Alexander have to suppress being alarmed.

"Well, this is most refreshing," Charlotte announced. "If anyone were to walk in and glimpse us all, they would think that they were coming upon two engaged couples."

This announcement made Darcy and I stop chuckling, and we grew suddenly nervous and began to mumble as we tried to struggle to consider what to say next.

"Well," I said, "we are keeping you and Alexander from speaking sweet nothings to each other. Captain, we must be quieter."

"Yes," Darcy agreed, "we ought to. Forgive us. Far be it from us to interrupt two people so much violently in love."

Darcy quickly untangled us from their company, and we remained on the other side of the room.

"You are fortunate to have a friend like Miss Lucas," Darcy said, for fear of having nothing else to say.

"Yes, I am fortunate," I said. "She forgives me, no matter what. I never understood her compassion for my sisters and I, since we are not on her level of beauty or society, but I shall not look a gift horse in the mouth."

"You think yourself plain?"

"I am. I am not afraid of that impression."

"I do not think so. Your looks are merely unconventional. But that signifies nothing."

"Thank you very much for that, and I appreciate the praise. But I do not regret being an average sort of woman. It has led to me being below certain people's notice that I do not want. Besides, as you say, I do lack convention, and that has led to me understanding animation. My younger sister, Kitty, is also that way."

"And what of your other sister?"

"Jane? She is the sweetest person in the world, but her sedate disposition does not lead to her getting the notice that she deserves. But Charlotte—"

When looking at Charlotte, I came to a realization. When leaving this house, I would do right by her.

"Captain, do you really have no say at all in this quartering?" I asked. "The lack of wisdom in having officers stored at Lucas Lodge is incorrect. You know it does not help your suit."

"I may be a captain, but my influence only stretches on the battlefield."

"I—" I lowered my voice, to the place of a whisper. "I am leaving this house. Therefore, there is no reason to monitor this place. The danger is going to move to the Green Dragon."

"That still is not enough of a reason."

And it was not. After all, Gage and other officers stationed in Boston were unaware of my existence, perhaps. But I had learned something from Darcy: trickery. And sometimes, a person needed a selfish reason to right a wrong.

"Darcy," I said, my tone gentle, because now it suited me to be more feminine in my tone. "I think it best to do something that will help the matter."

"You will stay here?"

"No," I responded, amazed that he thought so. "That does

not help things. My staying here will only make things worse. No, what I am about to offer is a trade."

Darcy drummed his fingers against his knee, absent-mindedly.

"A trade?" he repeated.

"Yes. A trade."

"You have my interest."

"If you can convince General Gage to remove the British from Lucas Lodge, then, on the soul of my parents, I will not argue with you about any matter, for a week."

When hearing that, Darcy's eyes lit up. In his look, I saw all the possibilities! Immediately, I regretted my offer.

"A whole week?!" he repeated.

"A day," I rushed out, to correct my blunder.

"No, you said a week."

"I ought to have said a day."

"Well, you did not. You said a week. And I hold you to it."

Groaning inwardly, I ground my teeth and closed my eyes.

"I walked myself into that blunder, didn't I?" I realized.

"Yes, you did," Darcy said, amused. "It was like watching someone walk to a cliff and then willingly jump over it."

I sighed.

"Well, there is nothing else for it. Do we have a deal?"

"Should we shake hands on the bargain?"

I arched my eyebrow.

"You shake hands with a woman? I am not against it, but I just thought you would be."

"In every other circumstance, I would find it vulgar to shake hands with a woman, but not in this situation."

He raised out his hand.

I placed mine in his and he shook it. When our hands were clasped, there was a sense of electricity between us, that ignited at the touch and we both felt it. It was nothing short of a quickening. Our spirits were more alert, a rush of euphoria had ignited between us, and it felt as if a warm fire had wrapped around our skin and encircled this one moment of unity.

We said nothing.

Perhaps it was because we were both afraid of saying anything, for fear of what this reaction signified.

"We have a deal," he said.

I released his hand.

However, he refused to let go of mine.

"Captain," I reprimanded.

"I just forgot to mention something earlier," he said.

"Whatever it is, you do not need my hand to say it."

He still held my hand.

"I am staying for dinner. So, you have to put up with my company for at least three more hours. Therefore, you may start agreeing with everything that I say now."

"First," I corrected, "I said that I would never argue with you, but that does not mean that I have to blindly agree with everything. Secondly, I said that I will not argue with you when you achieve convincing General Gage. Only then will the bargain be complete. And thirdly, three more hours?"

"Yes, Elizabeth, *three* whole *hours*."

I bit my lip.

"You are proficient at chess, aren't you?"

"Lizzy, I am the very best."

"I thought as much."

CHAPTER 19

How the Heart Betrays Itself

T hroughout the Lucas Lodge dinner, there were many observers, and much to be observed. Of course, there was a great deal of conversation that was ease and comfortable, and a few awkward silences here and there, but still!

Elizabeth and Captain Darcy were unable to speak a lot to each other, while still actively watching what the other had done.

Charlotte and Alexander MacDougall talked with gusto, but they did not just mark each other.

Out of the corner of their eyes, they rarely ever stopped watching Darcy and Lizzy.

Charlotte watched with approval and talked animatedly with Alexander about how happy she was to see her friend get along with the valiant British officers. After all, Charlotte was wholly unaware that Alex knew of Elizabeth's patriotic sympathies. Just as Alex was unaware that Charlotte knew that her friend was a patriot. Alex looked as well and could not share his fiancée's enthusiasm. He looked and was worried about the trouble that this would lead to.

Sir William and Lady Lucas had no choice but to watch as well, and both could not help but wonder if a match would be made soon.

Maria Lucas was doing her best to appear healthy, so she did not have sufficient time to watch too much.

Henry Lucas had nothing to say because he was not there. He was dining out with the British officers that were staying at Lucas Lodge.

But there was another person in the party who was watching more acutely. No one would have suspected him, because he was of such ease and light manners that he was often not suspected at being expert at observing others...

... and Sergeant Bingley had not waited long after they had returned to General Gage's headquarters to inquire to his superior.

But not as a superior.

Rather, as a man to a man.

"Captain," Bingley said as Darcy was retiring to his bedroom.

"Yes?" Darcy responded, with a candle in his hand. "It is late, Bingley. Can this wait till morning?"

"Sir, what I must talk to you about is not a matter of professional news. It's a personal sort of thing. If you do not mind me speaking so."

"Oh," Darcy said, unalarmed by this. "Very well. Come in then."

Bingley followed Darcy inside his room, as a servant was tending to the fire and arranging the bedwarmer.

"Leave us, Watson," Darcy told the servant, "And come back when I ring the bell for you."

"Very good, sir."

Watson left them alone as Darcy began to remove his boots and take off his military coat.

"Do you know," Darcy said, "my father once made a joke that he would never envision one of his sons in a redcoat. And then I had to go and upset him."

"My father was not so different," Bingley responded, standing at attention.

Seeing it, Darcy did not see the reason for it. After all, the evening had proven very diverting, and his spirits were still alight from Elizabeth's company.

"At ease, Bingley. There is no need to stand on ceremony anymore."

Bingley relaxed immediately.

"Thank you, Captain."

Bingley's face filled with worry, and Darcy noticed it as he removed his necktie.

"Are you well?"

"Oh, my face looks worried, does it not?"

"It does, indeed." Suppose it to be the joys of the moment, but Darcy had suddenly found himself to be very observant.

"Are you thinking of your late wife? Is that what you need to talk of?"

"You are willing to hear me talk of her?" Bingley asked, hopeful.

"When we first met, I did not think that it was correct for me to do so. But we are more acquainted, and now I feel that I can."

"Thank you, sir," Bingley said, his shoulders relaxing, because he was happy that his captain was learning to care for him. "I would love to talk about her. She was so beautiful, in her own way. She also loved to hum whenever she sewed. She was also very interested in learning about animals." Bingley

231

laughed. "I felt that, if she had her power, she would have wanted to have a menagerie. And if society had permitted, I bet she would have wanted to go to Africa and learn about the wildlife." His eyes grew sad. "I miss her. Faith, I am sick of how much I miss her."

"It shows proper feeling."

"It does. And nothing I say will ever bring her back. That is the pain of it. To be a man in love and have no power to keep the lady. And I—" Bingley cut himself off. "I ramble on."

"I was not upset over it. I understood, Charles."

"Thank you. However, I was being selfish because I came to talk about something else."

"What else then?"

"About you, captain. About your growing admiration for Miss Elizabeth Bennet."

When hearing Bingley announce such, Darcy's eyes turned cold, feeling the offense of his subordinate being so direct.

"That is too bold to speak of, Bingley."

"I am sorry, sir. But I felt that, perhaps, you did not wish to speak as a captain to a sergeant. But as a man to another. I thought it would help."

"Oh," Darcy responded, a little aghast. He was humbled by the appeal, that it had disconcerted him. "Thank you. It's just… it is not customary to speak so."

"Then you do not want to talk about her?"

Darcy leaned back in the armchair and rubbed his eyes.

"Faith, I do. I truly do."

Bingley walked up to him, slowly, and sat down in the opposite chair.

"I have been in love," Bingley said. "So, I flatter myself

that I can see when another man is beginning to entertain the emotion. And I see it in you when you speak to Miss Bennet. Am I wrong?"

Darcy did not speak, but that was admission enough.

"Yes," Bingley furthered, "I thought I was correct. I understand why, if it helps. She has a touch of sublimity to her nature."

"She does," Darcy whispered, angry, "and that is the pain of it. I cannot look away from her, despite that the match has nothing to recommend it. She argues with me, our tastes are entirely different, she is a poor colonist, and I am a loyal servant of the empire. She questions, she doubts, she is argumentative—"

"And she rebels against our being here, does she not? Or am I wrong? From the little that I have seen of her, I cannot help but suspect that she is patriotic to the colonies."

"She does. She sympathizes with the colonies' fight for equality in Parliament and the eyes of the king."

"She is a woman, though. Even here, her voice does not carry any weight. As cruel as it is to say such, but it is true."

"That is what I thought. No one listens to women. But I listen to her. Me? A captain of His Majesty's service. If I listen to her, then who wouldn't?"

"True. She has a fire to her. It makes her most rebellious tones to be charming."

"Precisely!" Darcy hissed. "She is charming. But true. Her charm is real and not false."

Darcy stood up and began to run his hands through his hair.

"I am falling in love with her, aren't I?"

"Yes."

"By rights, I ought to distance myself from her, for the sake of saving my own sanity."

"But it is hard," Bingley empathized, "to remove yourself from a woman that you are drawn to."

"Precisely."

"My wife had that same draw, so I know that all I can do is advise you to see little of her, but I know that you are not. And I will understand if you see her every day."

"I am not in danger of letting my affections for her influence doing my duty. For duty is the most important thing in the world for me. No, it is merely something worse."

"What?"

"That I am falling in love with a woman who I know, one day, will betray everything that I stand for."

Bingley shrunk a little under this revelation.

"Oh, good God."

"Yes," Darcy professed. "I might very well fall in love with a woman who will betray me. I am terrified."

CHAPTER 20

Another Betrayed Sensibility

"You do not have to leave!" Charlotte cried as I was packing away my items, so that I could relocate to the Green Dragon the next day.

After the dinner, I had told the entire Lucas family of my leaving. I had to deal with many protestations of my going, but soon, they died down when realizing that it was best.

After all, as I put it, 'one less mouth to feed'.

Of course, Maria and Charlotte were upset, but Maria understood why. Charlotte, however, would not rest until I went back on my plans.

"My dear Charlotte," I said, making sure that I had packed away all my stockings, "it is all settled. I promise that I will not see you all any less and visit often. Besides, it will do well, for you and for myself, for me to be on my own until I return to Philadelphia. Which I must do. I will not have you be tainted."

Charlotte took my hand to stop and steady me.

"Are you really to return to Philadelphia?"

"Of course, I ought to."

Charlotte gave me a knowing look.

"You know to what I refer? Lizzy, I am not blind. I saw the way that the captain looked at you. Darcy."

In spite of it, my fickle heart took a leap against my ribs. "We talk," I said, "but that means nothing."

"It means everything. You both—there is a connection. Only a person who does not understand the heart, would not see it. He is exceedingly fond of you."

"A man can be fond of a woman and not be in love with her. I have seen it before."

"As have I, however, it does not change that I am right."

"Charlotte—"

"Lizzy, are you really going to deny the reality of this? If you do, then I will not let you. Darcy is in love with you. Or if it is fondness, believe me, it will grow to love very quickly."

"I am a poor catch for him."

"It will not stop him, in the end."

"However, I am a patriot, and he knows it. Do you want this because you hope that he will reform me?"

"I confess that I would like that. But that is not prejudice, in support of the suit. Look me in the eye, Lizzy, and tell me that I am wrong? Tell me that he is not falling in love with you and that you are not feeling a tenderness toward him?"

Looking in her eyes, I was reminded of Dr. Warren, who also informed me of the same thing.

Both people's words began to sink in, and I began to understand—and accept.

I stood and moved away from Charlotte, placing my hands at my waist, and steadying myself.

The events of the last few weeks seemed to encircle me as I felt the quickening rush through my veins.

I shuddered as Darcy's image rose to my mind and came crashing down before my confidence, making me uneasy.

Immediately I tried to tell myself the reverse, and all the

obstacles that made this prospect unworthy.

We disagreed on every score.

We provoked each other.

We antagonized each other.

When looking at the other, we often saw the flaws.

But I always felt a joy in his presence.

A desire to see him.

And yet, I knew that this was wrong, because of the gulf between us, and where our path lay.

"You are right," I acknowledged. "Charlotte, your eye is as sharp as ever. He might feel all that you say, and it might weaken my resolve. Perhaps I might have no choice but to fall in love with him as well. My heart would not be wise and allow me to do otherwise. But I must leave eventually, for one obvious reason."

"And what reason would that be?" Charlotte asked.

"That this road could lead to only one outcome… that I would fall in love with a man who would have no choice but to accuse me of treason… and throw me into prison."

"What?!"

"That the man I love will have no choice but to brand me a criminal and watch me be destroyed."

By all, how did it come to this?

End of Book I

❧

Coming Spring 2024
Romance & Revolution Book 2

❧

Don't miss out on your next favorite book!

Join the Satin Romance mailing list
www.satinromance.com/mail.html

Hello Reader,

Welcome to the Afterword, where I am certain that you might have a few questions, concerns, and perhaps even bitter remarks about the choices that are made in this book and will continue to be made in this series.

No doubt, I made choices in this tale that were both shocking, as well as were uncommon for Austenesque fiction. I wish to inform the reader of why I did such, beginning from lighter inspiration to more serious subjects, and to encourage the reader of what is on the horizon.

Either way, I thank you very much for reading this work, and now, I hope this explanation interests you.

Inspiration

What inspired me to write this work? Well, this is the interesting part of it. When it comes to Austenesque fiction, I always enjoy writing the character of Kitty Bennet. I am a strange sort and find her to be quite fascinating. Well, in a previous series of mine, I had Kitty begin to become a writer—a habit I often do with her. In that tetralogy, 'Chance Encounter', Kitty began to consider writing a book called Romance & Revolution, about a heroine in America who falls in love with a British officer during the American Revolution.

Well, I took that idea that I gave her, and wrote the first chapter of this saga. Also, I did something that I had never done before: gone Meta. When writing this tale, I began to write it in the way that Kitty Bennet would have. In another series that I wrote, I had written Kitty to be very unafraid of the horrors of life. She did not fear seeing life at its best and at its very worst. From the injustices of the world, to the beauties of it, she was willing to accept the roller coaster of life. Also, she was not the sort who tried to rewrite history just because it was inconvenient of her to learn about certain realities. On the contrary, she faced it with fortitude and courage.

So, I wrote this as a Bennet sister writing about another.

As such, I was myself, writing Kitty to come up with an idea, then I took the idea and wrote this from Kitty's perspective.

I know that sounds very strange, but I think it helped carry me through as I typed.

Pride & Prejudice… and Science Fiction

Time travel and science fiction elements are not strange to Jane Austen's fandom world at all.

I liked the idea of Elizabeth and Mr. Darcy meeting and re-meeting each other throughout the centuries, in different incarnations and encounters, with one ultimate outcome. It was history repeating itself, while being entirely new.

Also, I love Sci-fi and Time Travel tales. I barely go a month without watching Star Trek, or another brilliant Sci-fi show/film.

And having the story open with Elizabeth watching the shows 'Quantum Leap' and 'Forever', was a foreshadow of what would occur next, as the series unfolded. Both were shows that had a profound influence on me and served as inspiration.

Actual Historical Characters

This book has its share of fictional characters, but there are also historical characters that did exist. Some were there at the moment, and others will be introduced later and serve throughout the narrative. These characters are:

Captain Preston – the actual captain who was at the Boston Massacre.

Dr. Joseph Warren – a Boston doctor, one of the Sons of Liberty, who serves in the American Revolution.

General Gage – the head military General, a French and Indian War hero, who enforced the Coercive Acts.

Lydia Darragh, Elizabeth Drinker, Mary Ludwig Hays, and Margaret Cochran Corbin – Four ladies who lived in Pennsylvania.

Lydia Darragh, Mary Hays, and Margaret Corbin – were patriots who served in the Revolution in a unique way. All women will appear later in the series.

Elizabeth Drinker – was neutral, with her family, but she kept a diary which was preserved, saved and has been published. Often, I pay tribute to her diary, because I used it as a reference guide as I wrote this book. Therefore, I thank that diary very much for being so useful.

Betsy Ross – the most famous of the ladies. She is often credited as sewing the first American flag. Despite historians doubting this, I will write her as being the woman who sewed the first American Flag, due to the circumstantial evidence that has been gathered of the event. I will elaborate on this in the afterword of a later book—if I have the good fortune for this series to be continued.

Alexander MacDougall – A Scotsman who was one of the Sons of Liberty.

Samuel Adams – one of the leading Sons of Liberty, and John Adams's cousin.

Alice – A slave woman, in Philadelphia, who really was a ferry woman who met William Penn when he founded Pennsylvania.

Samuel Nicholas – Nicholas, the man who employs Kitty, is a real tavern Keeper who plays a role in the American Revolution.

Esther Reed – a born and raised Englishwoman who becomes a patriot, and eventually is titled as a Daughter of Liberty and the Former First Lady of Pennsylvania.

The Growth Through Imperfection

And now for the most intense side of the tale:
    The imperfection of the lead and supporting characters.

I acknowledge that this was done deliberately for a set of reasons.
    First, it was historically accurate. As I will have one character realize in the next book: no one in this time of history has not been marred by the prejudices of their era. In that time, people were raised on such horrible practices, that it became second nature for them to feel such. And it was hard to see the error of their ways. Well, from a purely historical point, Elizabeth would have had mean feelings to the American Natives, because of her experiences, and ignoring the Tribes' experience. Darcy comes from a very wealthy family from Britain in the eighteenth century. Most of the wealthy families would have either owned slaves or profited from the slave trade, because the Trade fueled the wealth of many

national empires at the time, including the British Empire, and its Colonies.

Yes, I could have done the reverse and Darcys' family could have nothing to do with it. Or I could have left it out entirely. But it was a part of life. It was history.

Just like I could have left out the anti-Indian sentiments that were among the colonies and not given it to Elizabeth.

Why did I do this? Why make my hero and heroine so very flawed?

Because those were the times. Both individuals would have been shaped by the environment around them—the strife and conflict that was everywhere. As well as the prejudices from the previous generation that has bore down on them both since they were born.

Elizabeth was born into a land that belonged to the Native American tribes, and then colonization occurred, which completely destroyed the natives' way of living, and so, the Natives retaliated. Raids between both natives and colonists were frequent, and her family got caught in between this conflict. As a result, since she and others suffered from Indian raids, she does not see how the Natives were treated, and only sees things from her own perspective. Between that, and the way that the colonists viewed the natives, she would easily have this perspective.

And with Darcy, since he was a child, he was raised to believe that slavery was necessary to help Britain thrive, despite the injustice of it.

Also, it gives me the chance to have both characters change over time and confront the other's sins.

Elizabeth criticizes Darcy for owning people.

Darcy criticizes Elizabeth for being prejudiced against Natives.

As the series (if it has the chance) to progress, both characters will swiftly begin to realize that they were wrong. Darcy will gradually become an abolitionist. Elizabeth will go on to befriend natives in tribes. But the journey that both heroes go through is important. It's one thing to be born perfect, but it's another thing entirely to be raised imperfect, to *be imperfect,* and then realize that you were mistaken to believe such things is another thing entirely. It's evolution.

Also, Elizabeth's journey for revelation exemplifies the journey that the American colonies must take.

And Darcy's adventure for redemption exemplifies the path that the British Empire undergoes.

The pursuit of liberty, righting a wrong, and confronting one's mistakes, is a triumph of a significant sort.

It takes a strong ability to realize that one was wrong. Elizabeth and Darcy have that ability.

And lastly, it shows the complexity of the human spirit. And how no one is perfect, or all light and no dark. Or all dark and no light. That is not how the world works.

Of how two opposing ideas can exist at one time:

Darcy does not condone how the American tribes and natives were treated and will always have an instinct to shield them.

But he also is pro-slavery of the Africans.

Elizabeth is anti-slavery of ANY people.

But she mistrusts American Indians and refuses to like them.

Mr. Collins, like with Samuel Adams, has used the Sons of Liberty to take vicious action, sometimes even violent action, for his political beliefs. He has even tarred and feathered loyalists. Elizabeth was not there to see it, but he did so. However, he greatly respects women, never censures Elizabeth for speaking her mind, and would never deny her right to come and go as she pleases. If he were to see women walk down the street, demanding the right to vote, he would not take up the cause, but nor would he deny their right to protest, and even declare that they had a right to do so. He firmly believes that the female voice ought not to be suppressed.

Colonel Fitzwilliam is very idealistic and has many great qualities. However, he was as willing to turn his back on his family, without caring about all that they did for him. Mind you, he has a point.

And Elizabeth was a Quaker, who was kicked out, because she spoke her mind and simply disagreed on some things that she had a right to disagree with. Meanwhile the Quaker faith was based on equality.

This is to show that within a person, an organization, or a country, there will always be conflicting ideas, and even hypocrisies in one form. Because of simple *human nature*.

And lastly, I wanted to give the reader something different than what I have written and different to what I will go on to write. Diversity of subject delivery, as it were. It is also to do something cathartic. When it comes to readers, wanting something romantic and breezy is splendid, because it gives us a chance to dream away and are given a break from reality. That makes perfect sense, and those books serve a definite purpose. We all need to escape from time to time.

But there is also another side to a reader that has had a bad day, or a bad time in their life where they were not proud of what they were once like, and they need a set of heroes who underwent something similar. Sometimes, a flawed hero who evolves is precisely what another reader needs because that gives them the chance to say: 'oh, that's right. I am not alone. Others have been there as well'." It gives them a chance to confront something, and along with the character, they can overcome it.

I hope that I made the right choice here. I hope the reader enjoyed the first entry and will give me a chance for the second go around.

I hope to see you again!

Cheers,

Ney Mitch

THANK YOU FOR READING

～

Did you enjoy this book?

We invite you to leave a review at your favorite book site, such as Goodreads, Amazon, Barnes & Noble, etc.

DID YOU KNOW THAT LEAVING A REVIEW...

- Helps other readers find books they may enjoy.
- Gives you a chance to let your voice be heard.
- Gives authors recognition for their hard work.
- Doesn't have to be long. A sentence or two about why you liked the book will do.

About the Author

Ney Mitch has been a long-standing Jane Austen enthusiast, having written forty novels that were inspired by her various works. Since stumbling on Miss Austen's books after graduating from college, she has always dabbled in Austen inspired literature, ranging from writing works for teens to adults. Originally, her desire was to adapt Jane Austen's writing in a way to help young adults connect with her, however over time, she has spread her aims to other genres and styles. Having received her BA Degree at Desales University, she is a writer, both literary and dramatic, as well as being a Historic Reenactor.

 facebook.com/courtney.mitchell.589

 x.com/CMMitchelPsyche

 pinterest.com/shebaanna

Also by Ney Mitch

WITH SATIN ROMANCE

Romance & Revolution

The First Impression

❦

Kitty Bennet Adventure Series

Vanities and Vexations

Forms & Fashions

❦

Romance & Revolution Saga

The First Impression *(coming 2024!)*

❦

The Memory Series

Moments of Moments Past

Moments of Moments Present

Moments of Moments Future

Moments of Moments Infinite

❦

Pride & Prejudice Reimaginings

Rapture & Rebellion

Fortune & Misfortune

Desire & Destiny

Pride & Peace

Resolve & Revelations

Hope & Hopelessness

Chances Series

Chances Are

Chances Come

Chances Fade

Chances End

Novels

The Tale of Mr. & Mrs. Bennet: A Pride & Prejudice Christmas Tale

Considerations Near Christmastime